# Carly

## A STORY OF REDEMPTION

### Karen G. Bruce

Jan-Carol
Publishing, Inc
"every story needs a book"

Carly: A Story of Redemption
Written by Karen G. Bruce

Published August 2024
Little Creek Books
Imprint of Jan-Carol Publishing, Inc.
All rights reserved
Copyright © 2024 Karen G. Bruce

ISBN: 978-1-962561-35-8
Library of Congress Control Number: 2024944675

You may contact the publisher:
Jan-Carol Publishing, Inc.
PO Box 701
Johnson City, TN 37605
publisher@jancarolpublishing.com
www.jancarolpublishing.com

*I would like to dedicate this book to everyone who enjoyed*

*JOSIE: A STORY OF FORGIVENESS. I thought the story was done,*

*but the more I thought about it, the more I decided it wasn't over.*

*This book is a different journey and a different perspective.*

*My hope is that you will find your own redemption in God's amazing grace.*

# Author's Note

God is the ultimate musician. His music transforms your life. The notes of redemption rearrange your heart and restore your life. His songs of forgiveness, grace, reconciliation, truth, hope sovereignty, and love give you back your humanity and restore your identity.

— PAUL DAVID TRIPP

"Forgetfulness leads to exile; remembering is the key to redemption."

— Israel Baal Shem Tov

# Prologue

Carly walked through the cemetery where her mother was buried. She had not been to her mother's grave in over a year, the last time being with her boyfriend Tyler's mother, Josie, who had been her mother's best friend. That day gave Josie closure, but for Carly it only brought frustration and bitterness. She tried to get past all the hurt her mother and father had caused, but instead, her resentment had been escalating. Now, Carly was back. She had some unfinished business. It took everything she had to put one foot in front of the other. After her breakup with Tyler, she had nothing else to lose.

Carly tiptoed around the graves, careful not to step in the wrong place. Before she knew it, she was smack dab in the middle of someone's resting place. Was it wrong to walk across someone's grave?

"Sorry, Joseph and Harriet!"

Apparently, Joseph had died in 1965 and Harriet in 1975. There was a heart in the middle of their names and the caption, *Everlasting Love,* underneath. After all that Carly had been through, the idea of everlasting love was hard to understand. Couldn't anyone be honest and put, *Sometimes Love and a Little Hate Too?*

Josie had said that the grave marker had finally been put up and that she had placed the purple irises in the vase, her mom's favorite flower. She said it wouldn't be hard to miss, especially with a cascade of fall colors on all the other graves.

Seeing nothing but vibrant colors of orange, red, and yellow on the hillside, Carly was about to change her mind and leave when she saw the flowers she was looking for. She closed her eyes, took a deep breath, and then walked with purpose; the purpose of getting it over with. When she saw her mother's name, Shelly Francis Gibson, her heart began racing, and her stomach tensed. Taking deep breaths, she knelt with one hand on the stone and one holding her stomach. She wanted to pray, but she didn't know how. She wanted to talk to God about the rage she felt deep in her soul, but all she could say was *why?* How was she supposed to live a normal life knowing her father murdered her mother?

# Chapter 1
## *Carly*

Carly's first memories were of her mom and dad fighting. Boy, did they have some humdingers. If her dad said it was up, her mom said it was down. Carly had been a pawn in many of their fights. One of her earliest memories was when her dad, Jared, had placed her in the car seat in his truck. Before he could start the engine, her mom was jerking the truck door and pulling her out, screaming the whole time, "How dare you take my baby!"

Carly had been excited because her dad had said they were going to McDonald's, and she could order whatever she wanted. She was looking forward to chicken nuggets and a new toy. He would also let her play on the playground, which her mama never would because of all the germs. Her mama was a clean freak and was wiping and swiping all the time.

Carly began to cry because her parents were fighting, again, and she cried because she would not be getting any nuggets or a toy. Her dad followed them back in the house yelling, "She's my daughter too, and I'll take her wherever I want to take her!"

He also used a few unfamiliar words. Carly covered her ears and began screaming because she was frustrated and scared.

"Now look what you've done!" Her mother pulled Carly into her arms and tried to hug her, but it only made her cry louder. That was the first time Carly held her breath.

"Look what I've done? You're the one that's a crazy lunatic!" Jared said and began pacing back and forth in the large foyer of the house. The grand staircase was behind him, which led up to an impressive balcony with lots of decorative finishes. The house was spacious and full of natural light from all the expansive windows. Shelly was never happier than when people came over and bragged about how nice everything was. She loved all the oohing and aahing.

Shelly tried to hug her daughter again, but Carly only stiffened, making it awkward.

"You are such an idiot!" Shelly said. "Why do you think you can just take Carly without asking me first?" She looked down with concern at her daughter.

Jared also looked concerned. "Why is she turning purple?"

Instead of answering her husband, Shelly shook Carly. "Breathe, Carly! Stop that right now!"

Now that she had her parents' attention, Carly decided that she would make them pay for causing her such misery, otherwise, they would keep on fighting. The next thing she remembered was hearing her mother crying and her daddy saying, "I'm so sorry, baby, please wake up!"

Carly felt weak and confused. Not knowing what to say or do, she burst out crying again. Her parents were beside themselves, promising everything under the moon. Carly soon calmed down with all the petting and promises. At least their current argument was forgotten.

Things were better for a while. Everyone got along, and Carly was happy. Her parents seemed to love or at least like each other again. Of course, it didn't last. There would be many more knock-down-drag-out fights until they finally divorced when Carly was seven.

By that time, she was ready for them to go their separate ways. Shelly Mitchell became Shelly Gibson once again. She tried to talk Carly into changing her last name, too, but Carly thought that was stupid and told her no. She also wished she could drop her middle name, which happened to be the same as her mother and grandmother and beyond embarrassing. Besides, there was a boy in her class whose last name was Gibson, and she didn't like him. He liked to play with her hair, and she didn't want anyone touching her hair.

To say they were a dysfunctional family was an understatement. Carly had always wished for a sibling to commiserate with or even to share the extra attention. When they weren't fighting with each other, her parents would both be competing for her affections, suffocating her in the process. Christmases and birthdays could be so overwhelming that she didn't know if she should look forward to them or wish she should completely skip them. Each parent tried to outdo the other or they fought about custody and visitation. Other times, she would use the situation to get what she wanted, but Carly learned early that she would rather have two happy, loving parents than all the gifts in the world.

She often wished that her best friend, Tyler, was her brother instead. She loved his parents, Josie and John Carrier. She never saw them fight. Josie had been her mom's best friend since they were little girls, but they were nothing alike. Josie and John lived on a farm and had lots of animals. Her favorite was Judy, the cat. Once, when Judy had a litter of kittens, Carly begged and begged to have a kitten of her very own, but her mom wouldn't let her, because she didn't want cat hair all over the house. Josie said she could have one and keep it at the farm. It wasn't the same.

Every weekend that she stayed with her dad, they would always do the same thing. They would get some kind of fast food, shop for a new toy, and then rent a movie because he didn't know what else to do with his daughter. Usually, he was on the phone, because of his work as a contractor. Carly would often think of naughty things to do just to get his attention, like turning up the television so loud that he had to walk outside and finish his conversation. Sometimes he would talk to one of his girlfriends, which was even worse. In those cases, she took desperate measures like shaking up a can of soda and opening it so it would spew all over the kitchen.

At the beginning of any new relationship, the girlfriend would always be nice, trying to be Carly's best friend, but Carly didn't want a best friend. She just wanted to spend time with her daddy, and it didn't really matter what they did as long as they were together. Learning from her mother, Carly often lied to get her way, and the "GFs," as she often dubbed them, would be the recipient of her lies. Of course, the GFs didn't like that and figured out early on that Carly was their number one enemy. Usually, the relationships didn't last very long. Carly wasn't sure if it was her or her dad, but she really didn't care as long as they quit coming around.

When she was feeling mischievous, it was fun to create unusual ways to shock her dad's girlfriends, like telling them about her daddy's rude habits. Informing them about his morning constitutional routine was always a real revelation, especially when you added the part about how he would stink up the whole house. Carly liked to play pranks on one particular girlfriend, like putting fake poop on the kitchen floor, and laughing when she screamed.

Celine, who Carly dubbed "Saline of the Sea," was the jumpiest person she had ever seen. Carly intentionally mispronounced her name just because it irritated Celine, who thought she was a talented singer, and really, she was no better than a screeching seagull, hence, "Saline of the Sea."

For some reason, Carly's mother wanted to know every detail about the GFs, and Carly would often embellish, knowing it made her mother happy to know any little gossipy detail that didn't necessarily put them in a good light, like if they were a little pudgy or had buck teeth. Carly didn't like her mother's boyfriends either, but she wasn't around them as much. If Shelly had a date, Carly would usually stay with her grandmother and grandfather, or if she were lucky, with Josie and John.

Regina and Frank, aka Gigi and Pops, were not the ideal grandparents. Gigi smoked cigarettes, and Pops smoked cigars. They couldn't be around each other too long without fighting either. Pops couldn't do anything right, according to Gigi. You'd think after listening to her harp about leaving his clothes on the floor for a thousand years, he would pick them up occasionally. Instead, Pops went out of his way to annoy Gigi whenever he could, like leaving his sweat-stained, stinky ball caps on the furniture or saying he was going to take his car and get a "squirt of gas."

Pops had his mancave, where he watched football, smoked, and yelled at the announcers, referees, coaches, and players to his heart's content. His favorite was his alma mater, the University of Tennessee, where Phillip Fulmer and Peyton Manning were kings. He had posters, footballs, flags, helmets of every size, and glass beer mugs from one corner of the room to the other. Carly liked to watch football with him, getting excited when the band began playing "Rocky Top." They would both sing along, and sometimes she would march around the room while Pops laughed. He never let her leave the house without putting a little bit of "folding money" in her pocket telling her to buy a "little something purty."

Helena, their longtime housekeeper, often went around saying, "Qué lío!" whenever she entered the mancave. She would open the windows and spray disinfectant, all the while holding her nose. She would say, "Senor Geebson, it steenk like skunk in here!"

Pops would only laugh, trying to pat her behind. Helena would smack his hands and continue her tirade in Spanish. They didn't know what she was saying, but it had to be good stuff. Carly wanted to learn Spanish just for that reason. Helena smoked too, but only on her break and always outside.

Besides harping at Pops occasionally, Gigi lived in her own little world, which consisted of her daily consumption of menthol cigarettes, watching true crime television, and card nights with her bridge group. The Friday nights that Gigi hosted bridge night and Carly was there were often the best entertainment, better than one of her favorite shows, *Saved by the Bell*. One lady in particular, Nancy Bishop, was a character. Gigi would admonish her for saying bad words like s-h-i-t all the time, but Nancy said, "Shit ain't no bad word."

Apparently, it *was* a bad word when an eight-year-old said it.

When Pops, who was supposed to be watching Carly, would fall asleep in his chair, she would often eavesdrop, unbeknownst to all the ladies. Once they started playing cards, you never knew what they were going to say, which was the fun part. Even though a lot of their conversations went over Carly's head, she listened attentively.

Nancy had been married four times, and every marriage had been a disaster. She never had anything good to say about men, especially the ones she had been married to.

Her first husband, Dan Allgood, had been in the Army when they got married. He had been on leave and swept Nancy off her feet. Unfortunately, when her feet came back to earth, she realized that being married to an Army man wasn't for her. He came home earlier than expected one time and found her in bed with husband number two. Carly learned that sleeping with another man was not good. Apparently, they did more than sleep.

Robert Miller turned out to be a mama's boy, and Nancy couldn't abide that, so she kicked him to the curb too. She wasn't looking for number three, but Gary Ridgeway was so sweet and charmed his way into her life. Yes, he had the same name as a renowned serial killer, but he couldn't help that. He *could* help the fact that his bedroom skills left much to be desired. She thought she had given up on men completely until she met number four, George Nacht. George was Jewish, although secular or non-practicing, but really, he was an atheist if you wanted to know the truth about it. Nancy wasn't deeply religious by any means, but being married to someone that didn't believe in the Father, the Son, *and* the Holy Spirit was whacky. Nancy believed in the Almighty and didn't want to take any chances that George would bring her to the dark side. So, Nancy dropped the Allgood-Miller-Ridgeway-Nacht names and went back to plain old Nancy Bishop, denouncing men completely.

Bridge night was the beginning of Carly taking notes of all the happenings around her. Stories, especially ones from Nancy, were just too juicy not to write down. For example, Gary Ridgeway had a foot fetish. Carly had to look up what a fetish was in Gigi's encyclopedia. She read that *a fetish was a form of sexual desire in which gratification is strongly linked to a particular object or activity or a part of the body other than the sexual organs.*

Carly had to think about that one. She then looked up sexual desire, gratification, and sexual organs. She was very confused about it all and wondered what feet had to do with it.

Once, when Carly was being especially quiet, she heard Gigi talking about Pops. Apparently Pops liked Gigi to dress up like a nurse in the bedroom. She even had a white nurse's uniform in the back of her closet that Carly confirmed as being true. Why did Pops want Gigi to dress up like a nurse? Was he sick?

Carly didn't understand any of it, but she wrote it down for future reference. Sometimes, when she stayed at Josie and John's house, she would show her notes to Tyler.

# Chapter 2

## Carly

"Foot fetish?" Tyler looked confused. Carly pointed to her notes that she copied from the encyclopedia. He still looked puzzled. "I don't get it."

Carly closed her notebook. It wasn't that important, but she was curious and bored. "I don't either," she said. "Let's ask Matt."

Matt was always their go-to person when they were too embarrassed to ask their parents, like why the male ducks tried to drown the female ducks. Carly and Tyler both got red-faced when they found out that's how they made baby ducks.

Tyler hollered, "Matt!" When his brother didn't answer, he got up from the floor and went to Matt's bedroom across the hall, Carly following behind him. After banging on the door, he opened it to find Matt playing his video game with his headphones on.

Carly noticed Matt's annoyed look and was a bit intimidated, but Tyler forged right in. Carly gave the book to Tyler, and Tyler held it in front of Matt.

"What does this mean?" he asked.

Matt looked at the notes that Carly had written with a disgusted expression. "What is wrong with you two?"

Being the eldest, Matt often thought Carly and Tyler were beneath his notice, except when he was bored.

Tyler yelled, "Just tell us what it means, dumb butt!"

Matt pointed to the door. "Get out of my room, moron!"

Tyler rolled his eyes and headed for the door, Carly walking close behind him. Once they were back in Tyler's room, he said, "He doesn't know either."

Carly was disappointed because Matt was the only person she could think of asking. "I guess we'll never know," she said.

Carly sat down on Tyler's bed and stretched her bare feet out, looking at them closely. "What do you think about feet, Ty?" She spread her toes, noticing that her second toe was as long as her big toe. Was that normal?

Tyler had already pulled out his Legos and spread them on the carpet, picking out the blocks he wanted to start with. "What do you mean?" he asked.

Carly got up and held one of her feet up next to him, forcing him to take a good look. "Do you like feet?"

Tyler pushed her foot away. "Feet are feet."

Carly shrugged her shoulders. "I guess. I never really paid attention before except for when my dad needs to clip his toenails. Sometimes they can get really long and disgusting."

"You should see my dad's feet," Tyler said. "You can hear him all over the house when he clips his toenails. Sounds like he's shooting a gun or something. Mom says he could put an eye out with one of those things when they fly across the room."

They both giggled.

Carly sat down and began building her own Lego design, something they could both do for hours. That's what she loved about coming to Tyler's house. They had been friends for as long as she could remember. His parents were normal, or what Carly thought was normal. They didn't cuss each other or call each other names. They sat at the table for meals, and John always said a prayer before they ate while they held hands.

Carly would sometimes go to church with the Carriers. She and Tyler went to Sunday School together and learned about the Bible from Mrs. Waterman, who always made Carly feel welcome. One of her favorite stories was about Jonah, who didn't do what God wanted him to do so he got thrown in the sea and was swallowed by a gigantic fish. Jonah eventually had a second chance, saving the people of Nineveh, and was redeemed, even though he would be forever known as the prophet that disobeyed God. Carly loved the thought of second chances, like when she forgot her homework and the teacher gave her an extra day to turn it in.

Her mom sometimes took her to church where Gigi and Pops went, but it was quite different than Josie and John's country church. Matt and Tyler were both baptized in the river. Gigi and Pops thought that was the craziest thing they ever heard. They thought all you needed was a little sprinkle. They didn't go all the time anyway. Tyler practiced on Carly at the pool, and she thought being dunked was more fun.

Carly almost went to the altar at Tyler's church once. She wanted to be saved and baptized, but she figured she wasn't nice enough or good enough for God. Josie said that was the whole point, that you were never good enough, but Josie didn't see the dark side of Carly. She had lots of bad thoughts and sometimes hated her mom. God said you were supposed to love everyone, but most people got on her nerves. She knew she would just be a disappointment. Tyler had been saved a couple of times on account of him being sorry for something stupid he did, like the time he stole some candy from the Dollar General.

Tyler was the only person in the world she told her true thoughts to, and he didn't judge her or ridicule her. They went to the same school and were often in the same class. She was better at reading and spelling, but he was better at math and science. They had been playing soccer since they were in kindergarten. Tyler was better at kicking, but Carly could run faster.

Carly loved sports, which disappointed her mother to no end. Shelly entered Carly in beauty pageants when she was young, but Carly hated them. Her mother finally stopped when Carly stuck out her tongue and tooted on stage in the Young Miss Shenandoah pageant. Carly got a tongue-lashing from her mom, an eyeroll from Gigi, and a big belly laugh from Pops.

Since her mother was a hairdresser, she also wanted to fix her long dark hair, putting it in rollers and teasing it up. Carly wanted it straight or in a ponytail, something easy and simple. Besides, Tyler and Matt would laugh themselves into a frenzy when Shelly teased her hair. Carly was so mortified and angry when that happened that she chased them both and punched them in the stomach. Tyler's dad, John, laughed and said they deserved it.

Carly loved her mother, but the older she got, the more they didn't get along. Shelly was happy when she could dress her daughter in bows and ruffles. When Carly tried to tell her what she wanted and how she wanted to dress, her mother didn't understand. She thought that Carly should appreciate the fact that her own mother cared and wanted them both to dress up and do pageants together. To Shelly, it was the ultimate mother-daughter activity and part of the reason for having a daughter. If Carly heard it once, she heard it a million times: "Gigi never wanted to do anything with me. Gigi wouldn't even hug me."

That was true. Carly learned early to never hug Gigi because she didn't like to be touched. Carly was fine with that. She wasn't a big hugger either, besides, Gigi always smelled like an ashtray and stinky perfume. Shelly loved to hug, especially when she had a glass or three of wine. Carly hated those overwhelming, clingy hugs from her mother. The more she stiffened up, the more her mother held on until she was crying about what an ungrateful, hateful daughter she had. Carly wanted to tell her to stop, but she was clueless in relating this fact. She didn't have the verbal skills to tell her how uncomfortable she was. Carly knew that if she tried to tell her mother how she felt that it would only make matters worse. Usually the next day, Shelly would have forgotten it anyway.

Josie liked to hug, but she didn't do it in such a way to make Carly feel awkward. Shelly had complained to Josie, once, and in front of Carly, that her own daughter did not want to be hugged by her mother. She went on to say that Carly was just like Shelly's mother—a cold, unfeeling fish. Carly was embarrassed and furious. Before she could stop herself, she yelled at her mother, "I'd rather be a fish than a drunk!"

Later, Carly felt bad because her mother really wasn't a "drunk." She only drank sometimes, but to her, one time was too many. For a while, Carly tried to hug a little more, be a little warmer—anything but act like a fish. Josie told her not to worry about it, to just be herself. Eventually she did as Josie told her, but she never forgot it.

Carly held herself back from having any other friends besides Tyler and Matt. She didn't feel comfortable with anyone else. The boys liked her, especially Tyler, because she wasn't a girlie girl. Carly liked to play video games and sports, and she could hold her own. She could also burp and toot as loud, or louder, than the boys. To them, she wasn't a girl, just another friend that happened to be a girl. That was fine with Carly. She wanted them to treat her just like one of the guys.

# Chapter 3

## *Carly*

Carly was in the fifth grade when her dad decided to marry Gail, or as her mom called her, "Gail the Whale." Gail did have a big bottom, but Carly's mother did not have room to talk. Someone could have called her "Shelly the Big Belly," or something about her humongous boobs, which Carly prayed she would not inherit. Carly liked Gail, but every time she said something nice about her to her mother, Shelly had a fit. She would say things like, "She'll only be nice to you until she marries your father, and then she'll kick you to the curb."

Jared and Gail got married at the courthouse. They wanted Carly to attend the wedding, so her dad's parents came to pick her up and take her to the small wedding ceremony, against her mother's wishes. Carly didn't get to see Grandmother and Grandfather Osborne very often. They only lived about 45 minutes away in Fall Branch, Tennessee, where her father grew up, but they didn't drive much. Her grandfather had retired from Eastman, a huge chemical plant, in Kingsport. They had another son, her father's brother, who also lived in Fall Branch. He had kids, but they were all older than Carly. Carly saw her cousins sometimes at Christmas or other special holidays, but they weren't close.

After the wedding, they all went to Gail's house. Her sisters had decorated the small home and had tons of food set out for everyone. Gail's brother, Jackie, was also there. Carly couldn't help but notice him because he had a skirt on. She tried not to stare, but she was fascinated. He looked like a man, but instead of pants, he had a bright orange skirt along with a white dress shirt and a bright orange, checkered tie. He had on white tennis shoes with little orange puff balls on the back of his socks to finish the ensemble. She couldn't help but think that her Pops would be impressed. At least Jackie was color coordinated, and he was genuinely nice, carrying around cheese trays and telling everyone, "Get your cheese here! More cheese please!"

Gail had a daughter, Lauren, who was sixteen. Carly felt very awkward around her but did try to engage in a conversation.

"Where do you go to school?" Carly asked her.

Lauren looked annoyed but finally answered her, "Tennessee High School."

Lauren took a drink of her soda that was in a red, plastic cup and then placed it on the coffee table. It had condensation dripping, causing a ring around the cup. There were several rings already on the table, so Carly was fairly sure it wasn't a big deal. Her mom would have had a fit. They had coasters everywhere at their house.

"I wish I could go to Tennessee High School, but I have to go to John Battle," Carly said. Lauren didn't say anything, so Carly continued, "I just love the Viking Castle. It's so cool." Lauren continued to look bored, and Carly almost faltered but decided to give it one more try. "The maroon and white colors are so much cooler, and I'd much rather be a Viking than a Trojan."

Carly shrugged her shoulders for added effect.

Lauren picked up her cup and stood up. She said, "Good luck with that," before she walked out of the room.

Carly looked around to see if anyone was watching and noticed one of Gail's sisters. With a sympathetic, knowing look, she said, "Try not to let Lauren upset you, dear. She's had a rough time of late. I'm sure she'll come around."

Carly later learned that Lauren's father had been in a car wreck and died a couple of years before.

Carly nodded and began chewing the inside of her mouth nervously. Eventually, she got up and walked to the kitchen, picking up some of Jackie's cheese. She wasn't hungry but didn't know what else to do. Her stomach was already a little nauseous, and she regretted eating it at once. She walked out onto the back deck and sat down on one of the steps.

Eventually, her father found her and held out his hand. Carly took it, and they began walking around the backyard. It was small but fenced in. Gail had a little dog named Dexter, who Carly hadn't met yet. It was in Gail's bedroom because it was scared of strangers.

Her father began to explain to Carly that he would be living at Gail's house, which was on the Tennessee side of their small town in Bristol. Carly and her mom lived on the Virginia side.

"We're going to fix up a bedroom for you," he said. "It's a little small, but I'm sure you'll like it."

She would later find out that Gail wasn't too happy that Shelly got to live in the big fancy house, while they had to live in Gail's little house. Shelly got to keep her house until Carly graduated high school, and then she had to sell it and share the proceeds with her ex-husband. Jared didn't like it, but Shelly had a good divorce attorney, and there wasn't anything he could do.

Finally, it was time to leave the party, and her grandparents took her home. Carly sat in the back seat and closed her eyes. Thinking she was asleep, her grandmother whispered, "Gail seemed nice." Grandfather Osborne only grunted, but her grandmother continued, "Maybe this time will be better."

Carly felt sad. She knew her grandparents weren't fond of her mother, but Shelly wasn't fond of them either. The last time she was at their house, before her parents divorced, her mother got mad because they accused her of spending too much money. Her mother was furious. She accused them of being hoarders.

Her grandparents were definitely hoarders. They couldn't even bear the thought of throwing a plastic cup away. They had tons of stuff they took from restaurants, like ketchup packets, napkins, and straws, which were in piles all over the countertops and in the pantry. Shelly warned Carly to never eat anything there because it was either old or it had cat hairs in it. They did have a cat problem. They were everywhere, inside and out. Some of the cats looked like they were dying, with hair falling out. One cat, Bobo, had a really bad underbite. He had a tough time eating and usually ended up with cat food all over his whiskers.

Her own dad showed signs of hoarding, which aggravated her mom to no end. When they were married, they always got in fights because her dad would accuse her mom of throwing something away if he couldn't find it. Shelly liked everything neat and orderly. If she got tired of something, she got rid of it, and bought something else.

As soon as Carly got home after the wedding, Shelly wanted to know every detail. Carly answered most questions and told her about "Uncle Jackie." Carly tried to tell Shelly how nice he was, but her mother would have none of it and warned her never to talk to him again, that he may be some kind of pervert. After she went on and on about it, Carly got mad and said he wasn't a pervert even though she had no idea what that meant.

Shelly continued badgering her about the wedding and who was there until Carly yelled, "I don't know!"

Unfortunately, she had mentioned that she had a new stepsister, which was a huge mistake. Shelly began ranting and raving that Jared better not spend one dime on this girl, that he already had a daughter. Carly was so exasperated that she finally threw up her hands and stomped up the stairs, hoping for a little bit of solace in her bedroom. Sadly, her mother followed her.

Carly tried to shut the door in her mother's face, but Shelly pushed it open before it could close. "You better listen up, little girl. Your daddy tries to put on a big act for you, but he's evil through and through."

Carly was only 10 years old, but she had heard this rant a million times. She didn't believe for one minute that her daddy was evil. Shelly brought out the worst in Jared, but when it was just the two of them, her daddy was good to her. He would sometimes get distracted by work, but Carly tried to look over that. You know when someone loves you, and her daddy loved her. She was sick of her mom always putting her dad down.

Carly yelled, "Daddy is not evil!"

Carly pulled her dress over her head and threw it on the floor. Shelly immediately picked the dress up and walked to the closet, jerking a hanger out. "You don't know him like I do," she said. "He's done things, things that you couldn't even imagine."

Carly had heard that before too, but Shelly always stopped short, not willing to tell her daughter of the bad, terrible things her daddy had done. Carly sat on her fancy bed, with its huge canopy and draping gauzy material that her mom had bought for her eighth birthday. It cost a fortune, and Carly knew this because Shelly told her every time that she thought her daughter was being ungrateful. She hung her head because she didn't want to fight. She was tired. It had been a long day, and she just wanted to go to bed.

Shelly sat down on the bed too and put her arm around her. Carly began to stiffen automatically but willed herself to stop, not wanting to make her mother even more mad. She closed her eyes and prayed silently, "God, I really need you right now. Please help me."

She really didn't know how to pray and what to say except the way Josie told her. She said, "Just talk to Him like a friend."

Thankfully, her mother finally stopped her tirade. She knew that eventually Shelly would tell her all the terrible things that her father had done, but right now was not the time. Carly didn't want to know it anyway. Her dad didn't say terrible things about Shelly, even though there was probably plenty to say. He didn't complain about her or call her bad names, that Carly knew of. Carly knew her mother often provoked him, and she could see him turning red and look like he was ready to explode. He knew how much it upset Carly to see them fight and talk badly about each other. He tried to be a good dad, and for that, Carly loved him. She still loved her mom too, except when she was mad at her.

Once, when Carly had been particularly naughty on one of her weekends with her dad before he married Gail, he had spanked her. She was bored and walked outside in the backyard. There were tons of squirrels out behind his duplex. She had followed one and got distracted, going farther away than she realized. By the time she returned home, her father was furious. She would never forget the words that he said: "This is going to hurt me more than it's going to hurt you."

Carly couldn't actually remember the spanking, just the words. He said it was because he was so worried. Her mom had spanked her a few times, but she mostly just hollered.

Shelly, when she was in a good mood, was super fun. She liked to cook and would fix Carly's favorite meals like macaroni and cheese, spaghetti, and French toast. They would cook things together, including Christmas cookies, fudge, and gingerbread houses. Her mom didn't get to help with many field trips, except when they were on Mondays, but she always made special things for Carly's class like cupcakes, and they were not ordinary cupcakes. They were always the coolest and tasted better than anyone else's.

When Carly turned 10 years old, Shelly finally let her watch soap operas. She would tape *The Young and the Restless* every day, and they would watch Nikki, Victor, and others get into all kinds of shenanigans while eating dinner on trays in the living room. She would say things like, "Look at Nikki! She thinks she's the queen of England, but she's really just a has-been stripper," or, "If her lips get any bigger, they're going to explode on her face."

She critiqued everyone. They were either too fat, too thin, too much makeup, not enough makeup, pretty, ugly, or pretty ugly. She would fast-forward through the sexy parts, but Carly still learned a few things from that show. One, no one was ever content. Two, everyone had secrets. Three, people lie, all the time.

Gigi watched soap operas too, and they would talk about what was going on, like who broke up and who "hooked up." That was an unfamiliar word Carly learned, and she wrote it in her journal.

*Why do they call it hooking up?* Carly looked up the word "hook," and it had three different meanings: a piece of metal or other material, curved or bent back at an angle, for catching hold of or hanging things on; a thing designed to catch people's attention; and a curved cutting instrument, especially as used for reaping or shearing. It just didn't make sense.

Gigi thought Nikki was so glamorous and aspired to be just like her, except that Pops was no Victor, and although he made a comfortable living, he was nowhere near as rich. Carly thought Pops was better looking. Victor had a craggily face that no amount of money could fix. Gigi had pictures on the wall from their younger days, and they looked nice. Gigi said Pops used to be handsome until he got a fat belly, and Pops said Gigi had lost her bloom.

Gigi had been beautiful and glamorous, but now her skin was like leather. Her mom said it was from smoking and too much sun. Every time Carly fussed when Shelly lathered her up with sunscreen, she'd say, "You want to look like Gigi?"

Gigi also had a smoker's voice and extra wrinkles around her mouth. Shelly didn't usually smoke around Carly, but when she did, Carly would say in her most raspy voice, "You want to sound like Gigi?"

Shelly would roll her eyes and shake her head, exasperated. "What I want is a daughter without a smart mouth."

# Chapter 4

## Carly

*Dear Diary,*

*I got this diary for my birthday. I can't think of anything to say. Bye.*

*Dear Diary,*

*Today was a fun day at school. It was crazy hair day. Mom put my hair in a bun and had braids coming down all over, so it looked like an octopus was sitting on my head. She put googly eyes on the bun. Tyler got in trouble because he put red Jello on his hair when he got to school, and when he started sweating during gym class, red dye was running in his eyes.*

*Dear Diary,*

*I stayed all night with Dad and Gail last night. Lauren wasn't there because she spent the night with her friend, Leah. Gail is not a good cook. I gave some of my yucky chicken to Dexter under the table. He puked it up and Gail got mad.*

*Dear Diary,*

*Mom took me shopping for school clothes today and got mad at me. All I wanted was jeans and T-shirts in any color EXCEPT PURPLE! She was picking out miniskirts and ugly silk shirts. Yuck!*

*Dear Diary,*

*Gigi and Pops took me to the UT football game. Pops got a hot dog and spilled chili sauce all over his big belly when Peyton Manning threw the winning touchdown pass. I laughed, but Gigi said he was a slob, and she couldn't take him anywhere. The smell of hot dogs in the car was making me sick. We stayed at a hotel, and they had an indoor pool which was pretty cool. Pops had swimming trunks that had pink flamingos on them. He jumped in the pool and splashed Gigi. Her hair got all wet and was hanging in her eyes. I had to swim under the water because I was laughing so hard.*

*Dear Diary,*

*Tyler and I started a new club, but nobody wants to be in it but us. Matt said it was dumb because all we did was make up jokes, so we decided to make up jokes about him. Knock knock. Who's there? Matt. Matt who? Matt's a butthead. Tyler thought it was funny, but I thought it was pretty lame. I said it should be, "Matt's a stinky piece of cow turd stuck on a tractor," but Tyler said that was too long.*

*Dear Diary,*

*Our class went on a field trip to the zoo today. Tommy Temple got in trouble because he gave one of the monkeys some of his popcorn.*

The monkey got excited and started making all kinds of crazy noises and then started throwing poop! One of the zoo workers came over and fussed at Tommy. Ms. Jenkins said he would have detention when we got back to school. It was the best day ever!

Dear Diary,

Mom took me to see the movie, Clueless. It was okay, but I got aggravated because Mom kept saying, "As if." I told her she wasn't a teenager and to stop. She got mad and told me how ungrateful I was. Blah Blah Blah!

Dear Diary,

Gail was yelling at Dad the other night. They thought I was asleep, but I was spying on them. Dad was on the couch acting weird, so I ran in to help him. He kept telling me to go back to bed, that he was fine. He didn't sound fine. He looked really sleepy.

Dear Diary,

As if my life is not already a big pile of dog doo doo, Mom, Dad, and Gail all came to the school for parent/teacher conferences. They all got in a fight when the teacher said I had an attitude problem. Mom said it was Dad's fault and Dad said it was Mom's fault. I yelled and told them that I hated them all. Mrs. Shaw was extra nice to me the next day.

Dear Diary,

I have decided to run away. I've already packed my backpack with everything I'll need. I can't take it anymore.

# Chapter 5

## *Carly*

Friday was one of her mom's busiest days at the hair salon, besides Saturday, so Carly figured it would be as good a time as any to run away. It was also the only day Carly rode the bus home. The only soul she told was Tyler, and she swore him to secrecy. Before she headed out, she grabbed a soda and snacks for the road. She really had no idea where she was headed, but it didn't matter, as long as it was anywhere but home.

Carly didn't want to take a chance of being seen by anyone, so she got on the railroad tracks close to her neighborhood and decided to follow them wherever they led. Unfortunately, they led to some very dark areas of the woods. Carly began to get scared, especially when it turned dark. The temperature dropped, causing her to have violent shivers, and the night sounds were getting louder and louder. She had never been that scared of the dark until she was in the middle of nowhere, all by herself.

Carly began to realize that running away was not the smartest move she had ever made. She didn't have a real plan, other than getting away from home, and her home was beginning to look better and better. She had already eaten all of her snacks and drank the grape soda she had packed. She tried to think of her mom and all of the reasons she was mad at her. Instead, she remembered that Fridays were pizza nights, and they always ordered dessert to go with it. Her mom also let her stay up until midnight if she wanted to. They would watch a movie in her mom's bed, where Carly would always fall asleep. Their favorite movies were horror, so they had watched *Scream* and *Scream 2* the past two Fridays. What had she been thinking of when she decided to run away at night? She would probably get slashed to death, and no one would ever find her body. Carly kept imagining the scary, white mask from the movies. Between her nerves and the cold, she was close to shaking herself to death.

Carly sat down on the track, feeling anxious and sorry for herself. Her flashlight, which had been bright and helpful at first, was beginning to fade. She took the batteries out and then put them back in like she had seen her dad do when they had camped in their tent in Gail's backyard. The light was a little brighter, so Carly got back up and began walking back the way she had come. Boy, was her mom going to be mad. She glanced down at her watch to see what time it was. It was only seven o'clock. Maybe she could get home before her mom did, but she doubted it.

Carly should have called her when she got home, like she always did, but she forgot because she was in a hurry to begin her adventure. Her mom would be so worried. She began to berate herself on the dumb idea of running away, and then the flashlight stopped working completely. There she was, in the middle of nowhere, in the cold and dark night, not a streetlamp in sight. Now what was she going to do? She couldn't remember how far she had walked, but thankfully there was a little bit of moonlight to help her see enough to stay on the tracks.

As Carly strode on, weary and dejected with each step, she promised God that if He would help her get home safe, she would be good. She promised to be a better daughter and to be nice and not hateful at home and even school. She would hug her mom. As Carly alternately walked and prayed, she did not see one of the railway ties that jutted out farther than the rest. She tripped and fell, hitting her head on the rail, knocking herself out.

A rumbling sound and vibration finally woke her. Carly had no idea how long she had been lying there. She touched her forehead and felt something sticky and wet, but it was too dark to see what it was. When she began to realize where she was and that the sound and vibration was coming from an oncoming train, Carly got up as fast as she could. The bright light from the train blinded her, but she was able to get off the track safely. Unfortunately, she didn't realize that the side of the track was straight down a hill. She fell, scratching her face on briars and tree stumps all the way to the bottom until she finally came to a stop in a puddle of wet leaves.

Carly should have known better. Tyler had told her it was a bad idea to run away. Matt tried to run away once, and his dad found him before he got to the end of the road. He got yelled at and his mom cried. She should have listened, especially when she couldn't talk him into going with her. Carly began to shake uncontrollably. She slowly got up, wiping her forehead with her sleeve. She carefully trudged back up the hill until she got back to the train tracks, the train having already passed. She was a little disoriented and couldn't remember which way she had come and which way would take her back home. Carly remembered she had a compass at home that her dad had bought her for her last birthday. Why didn't she bring it? Carly felt something drip into her eye and then remembered she had an old T-shirt in her backpack. She took it out, wiped her face, and then shoved it back in.

Carly began walking in the direction she hoped would bring her home. Her head hurt, she was cold, and she was starving. She was thinking of pizza and Oreos when she saw a light ahead. Was that the street in her neighborhood? Carly began walking faster toward the light, hoping she was approaching home and things familiar. The closer Carly got, she realized that it wasn't a streetlight, but a flashlight because it was bobbing up and down. Someone was coming towards her.

Carly didn't know whether to be happy or scared. What if it was a bad person like she saw in the movie, *The Silence of the Lambs?* A weird, crazy guy could grab her, throw her in a van, and stick her in a well so he could cut off her skin and use it for…for whatever, she wasn't sure. Carly had bad dreams for weeks after secretly watching that movie with her stepsister, Lauren. Lauren laughed, but Carly could tell she was scared too. They both felt sorry for the creepy guy's little white poodle.

Carly stopped walking and stood still, trying to see the person holding the flashlight, but she could only see the bright light. Too bad her stupid flashlight stopped working. She slowly crouched down, trying to make herself invisible. The light landed on her, and Carly knew she was in trouble. Saying a prayer that once she died, she would go to heaven and not the bad place, Carly closed her eyes and waited.

"Are you Carly?"

Surprised, Carly looked up, but she still couldn't see the man behind the light that was blinding her. Just in case, she remained silent.

"I'm Officer Cooper. Are you okay?"

The man sounded nice, so she slowly got up. Carly tried to talk, but instead, a sob escaped her mouth, embarrassing her to death. She couldn't talk for crying, so the man stepped forward and crouched down in front of her, pointing the flashlight down toward the ground.

"It's okay, Carly. You're safe now. Everyone has been looking for you."

She confirmed that the man was wearing a uniform and that he really was a police officer. Between sobs, Carly finally managed to utter, "I'm sorry."

"It's okay, honey." The officer took Carly's hand, and they walked back down the tracks toward home. "You've got a pretty bad gash on your head. Does it hurt?"

Carly nodded. "Yes, a little."

"What happened?"

Carly tried to tell the officer what happened, but between shivering and hiccups, he could barely understand her. He told her they were close to the road where his car was, and then he would take her to the hospital to make sure she was okay. Once he put her in the police car, he grabbed a blanket from the trunk and wrapped it around her. After he started the car, he put the heat on full blast and radioed to dispatch that he had found Carly.

# Chapter 6

## *Shelly*

Shelly was a nervous wreck. When she didn't hear from Carly after school, she began to get anxious and finally canceled all of her afternoon appointments so she could go home and check on her. She looked everywhere, but her daughter was gone. After calling her best friend, Josie, she and her husband, John, came rushing over to help look for Carly, and she stayed at the house while they looked all over the neighborhood but couldn't find her.

They had just returned when she got the news that Carly had been found and taken to the hospital by a police officer. Josie was in the back seat of the car holding her hand, but John was looking at her in the rearview mirror. Josie was her best friend, but John was her true love. There would never be anyone else for her. He told her that he would never leave Josie, but Shelly would never give up. She had loved Josie since they were little girls, but she loved John too. What Josie didn't know was that Shelly had been with John intimately when he was in college. She had been his first, and if things turned out the way she hoped for, she would also be his last.

In high school, when Josie and John began dating, she couldn't understand what she saw in him. Yes, he was good looking, but he was quiet and didn't say much. The more time Shelly spent with him, the more she began to see what was so special about him. For one thing, he was more mature than the other boys in school. He never talked just to be talking. You could tell that whatever he said was thoughtful and important; people listened to what he had to say.

Shelly would always go to Josie when she had a problem or needed advice, but sometimes, John would be there, and he would always be willing to listen. She didn't think he would ever turn to her but one night, he finally did. That night was the best night of her life, and she would never forget it.

It happened after she had gotten into a fight with her boyfriend, Todd. She was bored, so she called her friend, Carol, and they decided to show up at John's dorm room at ETSU. She had never known John to drink, but he had been drinking that night. She could tell right away because he was more outgoing and talkative, and his friends were laughing at him.

When he became sleepy, she walked him to his room, tucking him in. They talked about everything but Josie. When he began to drift off, Shelly made the decision to slip into his bed, all the while saying soothing words. She loved him so much and couldn't believe she was lying next to him. Shelly caressed his hair and, because she couldn't stop herself, she began kissing his temple, down to his cheek and then lightly on his lips. When he began kissing her back, Shelly finally knew what heaven felt like. It was only the one time, but Shelly would dream about it for years to come. Sometimes, she felt guilty for betraying her best friend, but not enough to give up the dream of finally being with John.

Once they got to the hospital, the staff directed them to where they could find Carly. Someone had wrapped her in a blanket, and a bandage was covering her forehead. Shelly ran to her daughter, getting on her knees and crying hysterically.

"What happened, baby girl? I was so scared!"

A police officer and nurse were sitting on either side of Carly. The police officer spoke first: "I found her on the train tracks close to Robin

Lane. She tripped on the tracks, knocking her head, and then fell down the embankment."

"Why were you on the train tracks, for goodness' sake?" Shelly asked. Her daughter looked down guiltily. "It's okay, sweetie. Just tell me."

"I was running away," Carly said and squeezed her eyes shut, trying not to cry.

"Running away!?" Shelly put her finger under Carly's chin and lifted her face. "Look at me. Why were you running away?"

Carly sniffed loudly and began crying uncontrollably. "I...I...I don't know!"

Shelly pulled her daughter in her arms and hugged her close. "It's okay, baby. It's okay." Shelly looked at Josie and John, and then at the nurse. "Is she okay physically? What kind of injuries does she have?"

The nurse smiled reassuringly and said, "She's fine. She has a scalp hematoma on her forehead, otherwise known as a goose egg. She didn't need stitches, just a few surgical strips. She also has some scratches and slight bruising when she fell down the hill, but nothing serious. She was in shock, cold and hungry, but otherwise okay. We gave her crackers and a Sprite."

Shelly ran her fingers through Carly's hair and gently patted around her forehead. "Oh, honey, I'm so sorry," Shelly said and stood up. "Let's get you home." She turned to the officer and nurse. "Thank you so much for all of your help."

Before she could say anything else, Jared came bursting through the door. Shelly looked at him with annoyance, wondering how he knew Carly was at the hospital. The sheepish look Josie gave her confirmed her suspicions.

"What happened!?" Jared asked. Once he saw Carly, he ran to her, getting down on his knees. "Sweetheart! Are you okay?"

Carly nodded, her bottom lip jutting out. She sniffed a couple of times and fell into his arms. It was all Shelly could do to keep from bashing him over the head in annoyance.

"She's fine," Shelly said. She tried to keep it cool, but she could hear the irritation in her voice as she explained what the nurse had already said.

"Why in the world were you on the train tracks in the dark?"

Once again, Carly bowed her head and spoke softly, "I was running away."

"Running away?" Jared looked at Shelly with an accusatory glare. "Why was she running away? What did you do?"

"What did I do?" Shelly asked. "I was at work. Trying to earn a living is what I was doing."

Shelly closed her eyes and clenched her fists. If anyone could rile her to no end it was Jared Osborne, and she hated the very air he breathed. Things started going downhill right after they married while they were still on their honeymoon. After her first short marriage to Allen, she divorced him and vowed to never marry again, but Jared had seemed different. He was good looking, had money, and was actually a nice guy, or so she thought.

Jared had taken her to Cancun on their honeymoon. On the last day of their trip, Shelly discovered her husband's little stash of pills. He had pills to help him wake up, pills to make him sleep, and pills to help him perform. She didn't know what to think. She could understand and put up with all the pills except the one that helped him function in the bedroom. Well, that was just deception to the extreme. It wasn't like he was an old man. What was his problem? And Shelly, being Shelly, voiced her outrage and forbade him to ever use such measures again.

Once Shelly realized that his stamina wasn't caused by his lust for her but by a bunch of pills, she was incensed. Unfortunately, without them, their sex life was wretched. Shelly knew it couldn't be her, so she surmised that something in his past had wreaked havoc below the belt. She tried her best to figure out what was wrong with him so she could fix it and help their marriage, but every time she brought it up, he would clam up like an oyster. She bought sexy lingerie, talked dirty (which was humiliating to the extreme), and did everything else she could think of, but nothing seemed to work. She never told her best friend, Josie, about Jared's little problem because she didn't want anyone looking at her in pity or thinking she was the cause of it.

Fortunately, she finally became pregnant with Carly. She wished that her baby's father was John instead of Jared. It sure wasn't from a lack of trying. Josie would have been shocked if she knew the history Shelly had with her husband. Unfortunately, after that first time together when John was in college, she had never been able to entice him back to her arms or bed. Shelly would never give up on John, no matter how much she loved Josie, and she loved Josie dearly. Josie would never know how it hurt her to hear the sweet things John did for her. Shelly's smile never wavered when hearing intimate details about their marriage. One day, their picture-perfect marriage would falter. One day, her time would come. It would take patience and perseverance to get her just reward, and she was willing to wait for it.

Shelly finally opened her eyes and looked at Jared. "If you need to blame someone, look at your own self." Picking her pocketbook up off of the small table in the room, Shelly took Carly's hand. "You hardly have any time for your own daughter anymore. You're too busy with your new family and your *new* daughter." Shelly looked at Jared with venom in her eyes. "I heard that you're paying for Lauren's college education."

Shelly ushered Carly to the door, trying to escape the room before she punched him right on the nose. She said, "Make yourself useful and take care of the insurance information."

# Chapter 7

## *Carly*

*Dear Diary,*

*I ran away from home, and it was horrible. Besides itching from rolling in poison ivy, my parents hate each other even more than before. Now, when Mom can't pick me up, I have to go to Gigi and Pops' after school except when I go to Daddy's house. I don't know which is worse. Gigi won't let me even go outside to get some fresh air. I come home smelling like Gigi's Salem Menthol Cigarettes and Elizabeth Taylor's White Diamonds Perfume.*

*Pops had to tell me a million stories about when he ran away from home until Gigi told him to shut up, and not to give me anymore ideas. Daddy's house is not any better. He acts like he's mad at me but won't say anything. Gail is even worse. She acts like I should be in one of those homes for mean kids, like Brian Johnson. Brian used to be in our school, but they sent him off somewhere because he was always getting in trouble. Tyler said he stuffed all the toilets with paper towels and then Mr. Hyde, the janitor, got all mad because he had to clean up the mess. Tyler said he also tried to sell stuff like cigarettes and his mom's pills to anyone who had a little money and that he was sometimes drunk at school. He fell asleep in the library, and Mrs. Powell couldn't wake him up. I know I'm not perfect, but I'm no Brian Johnson.*

Dear Diary,

I was snooping around at Gigi and Pops' in the garage and found Mom's old scrapbook. I saw an album of pictures of her and Josie, and some of Tyler's dad, John. John's pictures had hearts drawn around them. That's so weird. It made me think of the time Mom and Daddy got in a huge fight. Daddy said Mom was in love with John. Mom said that Daddy would never be the man John was. He was so mad; I thought his head would pop off.

Dear Diary,

Katy Dillard was bragging about going to Disney World on spring break with her mom and dad. She said she got to dress up as a princess and meet Jasmine. I hate her. I'd rather meet the Genie anyway, or even Iago. They're much cooler. Mom said she would take me to Dollywood on her day off, but it rained.

Dear Diary,

Gigi and Pops took me to the mall. We had fun and they bought me new clothes. Everything was great until we were on our way home, and Pops spit out of the car. Gigi was mad and said Pops was vulgar and uncivilized. We played cards when we got home. Pops taught me how to play poker, and then I spent the night. Between Pops snoring and that stupid ding dong clock, I probably slept one hour.

Dear Diary,

I thought middle school was going to be great, but it's awful! I HATE EVERYBODY, except Tyler, and even he gets on my nerves sometimes.

He smacks his lips when he chews his food. I told him it was gross and to stop, which only made him smack his lips even louder. My teachers are pretty nice, except for my science teacher. She's old, nasty, and mean. Mr. White, the social studies teacher, has a huge mustache and sometimes he gets food in it. Every time he turns around, everyone is making fun of him. All the boys are pretending they have mustaches and they're grooming them.

*Dear Diary,*

I was snooping around in Lauren's room and found her diary. She's having S-E-X with her boyfriend, and she thought she was pregnant, but it was just a false alarm. Ashley, my friend at school, told me what S-E-X is and I'm NEVER doing that. EVER! I need to STOP SNOOPING!

*Dear Diary,*

It snowed last night, and everything is white. You can't even see the roads. School is closed! Yay! When they finally scraped the roads, Mom took me to the farm so I could go tubing with Tyler and Matt. The pastures were the best, except when you went over cow poop. Then, we went to Tyler's Mamaw's house, and she made us hot chocolate. She's always hugging us.

*Dear Diary,*

I'm so mad! Mom took $40 from my piggy bank and didn't even ask!

*Dear Diary,*

*We got a new Red Lobster in town! Gigi and Pops took me, and I ordered crab legs but didn't know how to crack them. Pops had to help me. They were so good when you dipped them in the melted butter.*

*Dear Diary,*

*There was a dance at school tonight. Mom and I got into a fight because I wouldn't wear the dress she picked out and also because I told her she could drop me off at the door but under no circumstances could she come in. I was sick to my stomach because I ate too many brownies and drank too much punch. Hardly anyone danced except for group dances like the Macarena. Ms. Stevens was making all of the boys get on the dance floor. They were hilarious.*

# Chapter 8

## *Carly*

On a Monday afternoon, Shelly picked up Carly from school. After a snack, Carly went upstairs to get her bedroom ready to finally be remodeled. She looked at the frilly gauze hanging from her bed and decided to yank it down. Her mom would not be happy about that, but she was sick of it. She heard the material rip, and it gave her such a satisfaction that she began pulling it all down. She wasn't a princess; far from it. Carly unrolled the poster that her dad let her buy at the mall and held it out. The Foo Fighters would look nice hanging on the wall over her bed.

Carly had been nagging her mother about changing her bedroom, and Shelly had finally relented. They were supposed to go to the hardware store today and pick out a color. She wondered if her mom would let her paint the room black. Probably not, but she would get the darkest color she could find. Any color besides purple. She hated purple and pink. Tyler said it looked like someone had vomited up Pepto Bismol all over her room.

Hearing her mother downstairs, Carly stuffed the gauzy material into a drawer. Her favorite football team was the Tennessee Titans, and she especially loved the light and dark blue colors. Watching football with her dad on Sundays was one of her favorite things to do. They both pulled for the Titans even when they didn't win.

Once she got her way with the colors, she would gradually add a few Titan posters. Her mother would hate it but too bad. Tyler would think it was cool, and he would also be jealous. Carly ran out of the room to see if her mom was ready to go buy paint for the walls.

Shelly was wiping the counters down in the kitchen. She said, "You know, you could clean up after yourself once in a while."

Carly looked a little sheepish. She had cookies earlier but hadn't noticed any crumbs on the counter. "Sorry. Can we go buy paint now?"

Her mother sighed dramatically. "I guess, but I don't see anything wrong with the way it looks now. Any girl would love to have a room like yours."

Carly turned around so her mother wouldn't see her eyes rolling in the back of her head. She had hated that room for so long and didn't care if other girls would love it. She didn't like it, and her mother didn't care one bit. All Shelly wanted was her way, all the time.

Carly took a deep breath and hoped they didn't have a huge fight. "I just want something different, Mom. Please don't be mad."

"Okay, fine, let's go get some paint, but I can tell you right now, I'm not getting anything black or close to it," Shelly said.

Carly smiled and headed towards the garage. "I promise I won't ask for black."

At the hardware store, it was touch and go for a while, but Carly was finally able to pick out colors that her mom approved of. She picked out navy blue and light blue, and Shelly didn't have a clue that they were Titan colors. Her mom would freak out when she realized how Carly wanted to decorate.

Their next stop was at Belk so they could buy new bedding to replace the old ones that were stuffed in trash bags in her closet. Carly thought they were going to have a fight right there in the bed and bath department. The poor salesperson was obviously uncomfortable and tried her best to find something they both liked. Before things got too serious,

Betty Baker, who must have been a hundred, showed them both a striped, soft, plush chenille comforter that was in shades of navy, white, and light blue. They all sighed in relief, especially poor Betty, when all parties gave the okay.

Carly balked at all the frou-frou extras, like decorative pillows, that her mom picked out but figured she knew when to pick her battles. As far as she was concerned, she had won the day with colors, and she was getting a new room. They both left Belk and decided to eat at one of their favorite restaurants, Bella's, which had the best pizza in town. After they stopped by Food City to get doughnuts in the bakery department, they headed home.

Once they got their fill of the sweet doughnuts and Shelly fussed about the extra pounds she had gained, they went upstairs with the new bedding and paint. Her mother eyed the pink and white gauze peeking out of the drawer that wouldn't shut.

"I could have saved that and used it for something else, you know," she said.

Carly looked guiltily at the mess. "I'm sorry, I just couldn't wait," she said. She pointed to the closet and trash bags filled with bedding. "I already tried to get as much out of the way as possible for the painters. When are they coming?"

"Tomorrow morning. I'm taking the day off." Shelly took the curtains down. "It's two fellas that Gigi and Pops recommended. I hope they do a decent job. Gigi said they're a little slow, but you can't beat the price. Help me move the bed out so we can vacuum under it."

After they cleaned the carpet and baseboards, they both sat down.

Carly begged, "Can I stay home tomorrow, too?"

"Absolutely not!" Shelly said. "You'll just be in the way. Hopefully, they can finish the room tomorrow, as long as they don't have to put too many coats on the wall."

"Okay." Carly looked around the room, glad this was the last day of "the pukey pink walls," which Tyler had dubbed them. "Thank you, Mom, for letting me redecorate my room." She didn't want to hug her mom but felt that her mom would be happy if she did, so she walked over and slipped her arm around her mom's waist.

Looking surprised, Shelly looked down at her daughter and smiled. "You're welcome, sweetie. I'm sorry it took so long."

Carly was glad for their special moment. It was the happiest she had felt in a long time. She asked, "Can you make some popcorn tonight so we can watch TV in bed?" They had already established that Carly would sleep in her mom's bed that night.

"Sure. I've already blown my diet, so why not? Anything special you want to watch?"

"Let's watch *My Girl*."

It was a favorite with both Shelly and Carly. Carly liked the actor who played Vada and thought they looked alike.

"Okay, but lights out by ten," Shelly said.

Carly went to bed with a smile on her face that night, but two days later, that smile was gone.

# Chapter 9

## *Carly*

Carly was neck deep in a tub of hot water. She had decided that was the only way she would feel clean again but was beginning to have her doubts. The painters hadn't finished painting her room on Tuesday and had to come back on Wednesday to finish the job. They were waiting on the driveway when Carly got off the bus. Her mom had given her instructions to let them in, and then to stay out of the way.

If only she had listened to her mother. If she had, she wouldn't be soaking in a tub, feeling like the dirtiest, most unclean person on the planet. She had been so excited about her room, and she couldn't stay away.

Gus and River were so nice—at least, Carly thought so at first. Gus was old, but River was cute and had the coolest name. Carly fell in love on the spot after he winked at her. She was trying to be helpful and offered sodas and snacks while they were there. She was standing in the pantry when it happened.

Carly was trying to decide what cookies the painters would want, when all of a sudden, she heard a noise. River was standing behind her, smiling. At first, she was caught off guard and smiled back, thinking how nice he was. The next thing she knew, she was cornered, and the vile man had his hands on her shoulders and then on her boobs. Carly was so shocked that she froze and couldn't seem to do anything when his mouth touched hers and his tongue came in her mouth. He tasted like nacho cheese Doritos that she had given him earlier, and Carly gagged.

Thankfully, Gus was there and pulled River off of her, saying, "What the hell are you doing!?"

River grinned. "Man, she was so ripe and asking for it."

While they argued, Carly brushed past them and went straight to her mom's room and locked the door. Carly blamed herself. Was she asking for it? He seemed nice, and she did think he was cute, but now she could only think of him as disgusting. Her mom was going to kill her. She would blame Carly and tell her that she never listened.

Once she heard the men leave, she went downstairs, locked the front door, and went back to her mother's room. She didn't even want to see her finished bedroom. At that moment, she couldn't have cared less. The only thing she wanted was to take a bath so she wouldn't feel so dirty.

Later, Carly began shaking uncontrollably in the cooled bath water. She would never forget the nasty taste of him. Carly had always been curious about kissing. After that experience, she never wanted to kiss anyone ever again.

Still shaking, Carly climbed out of the bathtub and toweled herself dry. She put her mom's big bathrobe on and then curled up in some throw blankets on her mom's bed, crying in the pillow.

Shelly finally came home from work and found Carly, still curled up, watching television. By that time, she had stopped crying, but her mom could tell something was wrong.

"What's wrong, honey? Are you okay?" Shelly asked.

Deciding that she didn't want her mom mad, Carly didn't tell her what happened. "I don't feel good. I think I'm getting sick."

"Getting sick?" Shelly felt Carly's forehead. "You do feel a little warm. Hope you don't have the flu." Her mom tucked the covers around Carly. "Do you want me to get you something to eat? I can make you a grilled cheese sandwich and heat up some tomato soup? That okay?"

Carly wasn't sure she could eat, but she nodded anyway. "Can you get my pajamas?" She didn't think she could go back to her room yet.

"Sure, honey," Shelly said. After picking out sleepwear and bringing it back to Carly, Shelly turned the bed down and fixed the pillows while she dressed. "I'll be downstairs fixing your dinner. Holler if you need anything."

Carly nodded. Sometimes she hated her mother, but other times, she felt as if her mother was the best person in the world, especially when she was sick or just didn't feel good. She knew she should tell her what happened, but she felt so ashamed. At that moment, she knew she couldn't tell her mom, or anyone else. Carly figured she was a bad person deep down, and she deserved it. Maybe, just as River said, she was ripe and asking for it, whatever that meant.

Sometimes you just had to keep things to yourself. Her mom loved her and would take care of her because she thought she was sick. If she knew what had really happened, Shelly wouldn't be so nice and understanding. Her mom would be saying, "I told you so." For once, Carly wished she had listened.

The thrill of having a new bedroom had vanished. She tried to act excited when it all came together, but as soon as the door closed, all she could see was River winking at her.

In the end, she hated her new bedroom and the memories it evoked, but she couldn't tell her mom that. She would just have to live with it, and she would also have to live with the shame. She hoped no one would find out. She didn't want anyone to find out that she had been groped and kissed by a nauseating, horrible man.

# Chapter 10

## Carly

Dear Diary,

I had a dream about R last night. He was chasing me, and I woke up before he caught me. Mom took me to the doctor because I kept complaining about my stomach hurting. Doctor Thomas said it was just nerves. Mom blames Dad, and Dad blames Mom for my nervous stomach. It's my fault and they should blame me, but I can't tell them that. If I ever see R again, I wish I had a gun because I would shoot him.

Dear Diary,

Tyler was acting all funny when I was at his house the other day. Josie had gone to the store to get milk and we were in his room watching Gremlins for the 50th time. When the movie was over, Tyler got closer to me and touched my hand. I looked at his hand and then at him in confusion. He was smiling and then leaned to kiss me. I wondered why he was chewing gum instead of chips. At first, I let him, and then I kept thinking of R and I pushed him away. He got mad, and I tried to act like it wasn't a big deal. I wanted to tell him about R, but I couldn't. Ever since, he's been acting all weird.

Dear Diary,

Middle school is almost over. I'm going to Dollywood with Dad and Gail. I'm going to ride every rollercoaster and eat as many funnel cakes as possible. Lauren was going to go to but changed her mind and went to Carowinds in North Carolina instead with her friends. One of Gail's sisters is going to keep Gail's dog, Dexter. He's got cancer and has to have some kind of shots. He's got big tumors all over his belly.

Dear Diary,

Pops is in the hospital. He had to have heart surgery. He said his old ticker is worn out. Gigi said that wasn't the only thing that was worn out. I think she's talking about his old jeans. She swears she's going to throw them in the garbage, but Pops said he would just dig them out again.

Dear Diary,

I tried out for cheerleader for high school but didn't make it. Michelle made it, which makes it worse, but I think Mom was more bummed than I was. Who wants to be a stuck-up cheerleader anyway?

Dear Diary,

John Battle High School is the coolest. Tyler and I are both on the cross-country team. It's so much fun after school, except for the part where my shins are on fire. I'm really good and can run faster than anyone on the team except for Michelle Wood. I hate her. If Tyler doesn't stop talking about her all the time, I'm going to trip her at our next meet if I see a good mud puddle. That should wipe the stupid smirk off of her face.

Dear Diary,

Tyler and Michelle like each other, and they make me sick.

Dear Diary,

Dad and Gail are getting a divorce. Gail was mostly nice except for that time I gave her dog chocolate and Dexter had to go to the vet and he almost died. Apparently, saying you're sorry is not good enough. I knew things weren't good when we went to Dollywood. They argued over everything. Dad is mad because he has to pay money to her after the divorce. He said between Mom and Gail, he didn't have a pot to piss in. I laughed, but he said it wasn't funny. I said he shouldn't say piss, and he told me to quit being cheeky. Dexter finally died.

Dear Diary,

I don't have to stay with Dad on the weekends for a while. Grandmother and Grandfather Osborne both got put in the nursing home on account of almost setting their house on fire because they can't remember anything, like turning off the stove. Dad moved into their house so he can fix it up and sell it. Mom says there's something shady going on over there. The last time I went to their house, I could barely get through the living room. Boxes and junk were everywhere. I wonder if Dad will feed all the cats that are still hanging around in the back yard. There's a million of them. I wanted to pet them, but they all ran away.

Dear Diary,

Michelle is so snooty. She thinks she's better than everyone else because her daddy is a doctor.

# Chapter 11

## *Shelly*

Shelly was worried about Carly. All she had talked about was fixing up her room, and now that it was finished just the way she wanted it, she could care less. At first, Shelly was frustrated and mad, but there was definitely something else going on. As usual, her errant daughter wouldn't tell her what it was. Josie told her that Tyler was acting weird too, that something may have happened between them.

Shelly wasn't sure if that was the case because Carly was acting afraid to stay by herself and would go ballistic if the doors weren't locked. If she tried to talk to her about it, Carly would just get mad and clam up. At least she didn't have to worry about her daughter running away again. Usually, she didn't listen to anything Jared had to say, but he did tell her that Carly usually liked to go with him to the jobsites but had refused lately. Normally, Shelly would be glad of that, but along with everything else, something didn't add up.

Shelly had even taken Carly to the doctor because she was constantly complaining of a bellyache. The doctor said it was probably just nerves. What did she have to be nervous about? She seemed to like her new school. She liked track and was doing well in her classes.

Before she came to work, Shelly dropped Carly off at Josie and John's house. She worked late the night before and she was tired. Shelly wished that, for once, she could have a Saturday off, just like everyone else, but

Saturdays were her busiest day. She couldn't afford to take the day off. She needed the money. Her dad, bless his heart, had given her some money to help with some unforeseen expenses at the shop that month. Her mom would have a cow if she found out.

Jenny, her part-time assistant at the salon, finished washing Myrtle's hair. Once she wrapped it in a towel, she sent her to Shelly's chair. Myrtle Thomas had had the same cut and style for as long as she could remember, along with her special blue rinse. She never missed her 10 o'clock appointment on Saturdays, except that time she had emergency gallbladder surgery. Ms. Myrtle gave her fifteen dollars and a one dollar tip every week, and an extra five dollars if she had it cut. Even though the prices were displayed on the fancy chalkboard where everyone could see, Myrtle had paid the same amount since 1990 when she first came to Shelly. Her old hairdresser had died.

Josie had decorated the chalkboard and wrote the prices in beautiful handwriting. Her shop had touches of Josie all over it. All Shelly had to do was say, "I was thinking," and Josie would come up with something new, and it would always be exactly what she was looking for.

Josie had seen a picture in a magazine of a wall covered in greenery and a lighted sign that said, "Hey, gorgeous!" Since John was an electrician, he did the sign, and Josie did all the rest. She didn't know what she would do without her best friend and John. Josie was her confidante, and John was her true love. He was always in her thoughts, and especially her dreams.

She couldn't help what she dreamed. They were always so vivid too. She knew it was wrong to covet her best friend's husband, but she couldn't help it. She loved him.

Shelly's mom always called her out on it too; she said she could see right through her. She'd stand there with that cigarette bobbing in her mouth and say, "What kind of friend are you, always lusting after someone else's husband?"

Every time Shelly lit her own cigarette, she would think of her mom and vow to quit, but it was easier said than done.

Josie and John had an appointment and were going to bring lunch. They had taken the kids to the skating rink and were going to drop Carly off at home later. She hoped they would bring a big ole greasy cheeseburger with everything on it. Saturdays were always crazy, and she needed something to last her until she could finally leave and pick up something to eat. Carly had already told her she wanted a roast beef sandwich for dinner.

Shelly had three calls that morning from clients that didn't have an appointment and were desperate to have their hair either cut or colored. She told them to come on and she'd try and work them in. Jenny, her assistant, was going to take care of the shop while she took a lunch break.

Since Jared had divorced Gail and had to put his parents in a nursing home, he had been complaining about money a lot. Shelly had no sympathy for him. He begged her to sell the house so they could split the profits. She actually laughed in his face and told him that she wasn't selling the house a day sooner than she had to. He would just have to suck it up. Knowing he couldn't do anything about it made Shelly feel all the better. There was nothing she enjoyed any better than provoking Jared in any way she could. Marrying him had been the biggest mistake of her life, and except for having Carly, she rued the day she had ever met him.

Thinking back to that day when she first met him and thought that he was as close to John as she could get infuriated her. In the end, the only thing going for him was his money, and even that wasn't enough to put up with all his garbage. How he hadn't been sued by everyone, including the IRS, was baffling. His floozy, Gail, finally figured him out and kicked him to the curb. Of course, Shelly had given her a few tips one day when she saw her in the grocery store, but she hadn't told her the worst of it. Nothing was more satisfying than telling Gail what a loser she was married to. She never saw a man more disgusting.

She'd never forget the first time she found out Jared had been having an affair. Shelly had been so upset and actually blamed herself. Maybe if she had tried harder, been more supportive and loving, he would never have stepped out on her. When she found out the other woman was a man, her world actually stopped spinning on its axis.

He said everything to try and make her forgive him, but from that moment on, she hated him with a passion greater than any love she had ever felt. She couldn't look at him without seeing a vile and nasty man who ruined her life. That was the one secret she couldn't tell anyone without it hurting her daughter. Carly deserved a better father, and she didn't deserve that baggage in her life. Sometimes, it took everything Shelly had not to tell her everything so Carly would know the truth.

Jared had every excuse in the world. A neighbor had lured him in and abused him when he was young. He tried so hard to stop and was sickened by what he did but continued to do it. He must have told her a thousand times that he wasn't gay. All she knew was that she had been tricked and duped into marrying a despicable man. He had ruined her life, and she would never forgive him.

As she was putting the last little touches of curl on Myrtle's head, the door chimed, and John walked in. Shelly couldn't help the smile that spread on her face. John was the man of all men. He was perfect in every way. She wondered what her life would have been like if she had been his girlfriend in high school instead of Josie. She wished that she had fallen in love with him first. He was still so handsome in a rugged sort of way. Today, he was wearing jeans and a green pullover that made his beautiful eyes shine and sparkle. Any girl would kill for his long eyelashes.

"Where's Josie?" Shelly asked.

"She's coming," John said. "She remembered that Carly's sweater was in the back of the car and went back for it." John placed the fast-food bags down and headed toward the customer chairs and picked up one of the men's magazines.

"Is it the blue one? We were looking for it the other day," Shelly said.

John shrugged. "I don't know." Before he could sit down, Josie was walking in, carrying the blue sweater.

"Carly left this a couple of weeks ago, but I kept forgetting it," Josie said and held up the sweater, placing it behind Shelly's counter.

Shelly took Myrtle's cape off. "You're all done, sugar. I guess I'll see you next week."

Myrtle fished in her pocket for money and placed it in the pocket of Shelly's work smock. "My perm didn't last very long this time," she said. "Next week, mark me down for one. You might want to try a different brand."

Shelly smiled through her teeth, biting her tongue from saying something she would regret.

Josie grabbed Myrtle's jacket off of the coat rack and said, "How are you, Ms. Myrtle? I made your buttermilk pound cake the other day, and John and the boys loved it so much it was gone in two days."

As Myrtle slipped her arms in the jacket sleeves, she smiled. "I'm hanging in there, Josie," she said. "Every day is a struggle, but I still have my independence. Glad your men loved the cake. I always liked to cook for my man. He loved his sweets. Of course, that's what killed him in the end. He turned fat and smothered to death. I tried to get him to eat less, but once he started, he couldn't stop." Myrtle looked pointedly at John and smirked. "Let that be a lesson to you, young man."

John nodded as she walked out the door. "Yes, ma'am."

Shelly and Josie both giggled.

John looked at the women, wondering why they were all amused at his expense. "For your information, I only had about two slices of that cake. The boys were the ones that ate it all."

Josie laughed out loud. "Those two slices were about half the cake."

John shook his head and opened the magazine again while Shelly and Josie went to the back of the shop with the food. Shelly pulled out paper plates and napkins and placed them on the small table.

"Grab whatever drinks y'all want," Shelly said. "I'll take anything diet."

Josie took the sodas out of the small refrigerator and placed them on the table. "What did the doctor say about Carly?" she asked.

Shelly sighed. "He said it was probably just nerves. Something is going on with her, but she won't tell me what. Jared probably did something to her, but she's protecting him." Shelly shook her head. "I swear, if that slimeball did anything to hurt my baby, I'm going to kill him and enjoy doing it."

"I asked Tyler if he knew anything, and he said he didn't," Josie said. "He was quick about answering, so I'm wondering if he's telling the truth." She opened her soda and took a drink. "I'm sure she's fine. Remember when you were in the fifth grade? Mary Beth Brown kept threatening to tell your mom that you had kissed Joe Fuller at the fall festival?"

Shelly sat down, opening her food wrapper. "I hated her! I was afraid she'd tattle on me and then I wouldn't have gotten to go on that ski trip with his family. My stomach was in knots every time I went home from school, afraid that Mom had found out. I can't imagine anything like that with Carly. I don't think she's ever even had a boyfriend. She's in the prime of her life, and I swear, instead of trying to look nice, she goes out of her way to look bad. She won't let me fix or cut her hair. She lets it fall in her face, and it always looks stringy. She wears the same sweatshirts and jeans every day that hide her body. She's getting the cutest little figure, and she doesn't want anyone to see it. If I looked like that when I was in high school, I would have had any boy I wanted."

Shelly and Josie both remembered their high school days when Shelly always wore the nicest, most fashionable clothes and the teeniest bikinis. She did have lots of boyfriends, but not the kind that lasted. They were usually after only one thing.

Remembering Josie's mom, Shelly asked her, "How's your mom doing?"

Josie shook her head. "Not good. She's so weak from all the cancer treatments. If it doesn't work, I don't know what we'll do. I'm so scared that she's not going to make it."

Shelly had always been jealous of Josie and her mom. They had been as close as a daughter and mother could ever be. There wasn't anything Mrs. Taylor wouldn't do for her family. Shelly had always wished that she could have had a relationship like that with her mom. After spending the night with Josie when they were little girls, Shelly would go home and try to hug her mother. Instead of hugging Shelly back, her mother would suddenly remember something she had to do, like reorganize the kitchen pantry or call her friends to organize their get-togethers.

If Shelly said anything, Gina would admonish her daughter and often made her feel that she was upset over nothing. She'd say, "I'm just not a hugger! It's no big deal."

Shelly knew her mother loved her in her own way, but it wasn't enough for a little girl starving for affection.

# Chapter 12

## Carly

*Dear Diary,*

*I love the library. Ms. Jones has shown me all kinds of mystery books, which are my favorite. I've been reading at least a couple of books every week.*

*Dear Diary,*

*Tyler and Michelle broke up. Apparently, Michelle is a jealous goose and can't stand that his best friend is a girl. Me! I finally told him what happened with R and swore him to secrecy. He promised me he would never tell, and he's been extra nice. So nice that Michelle had a fit and told him that it was her or me. I guess he picked me, because she broke up with him. Now she's trying to get everyone to hate me by saying I'm weird. I don't care if they all hate me as long as Tyler is my friend. I am a little weird, but I'd rather be weird than a stuck-up Barbie doll.*

*Dear Diary,*

*Dad took me to see Grandmother and Grandfather Osborne in the nursing home. I almost gagged when we got there. It smelled like pee. Their room had two small beds to sleep in. They had pictures on the wall* of the family, and you could see a bird feeder outside their window. I saw a cardinal eating birdseed and remembered that they used to laugh at me because I called them Red Jays when I was little. Grandmother talked a lot, but Grandfather didn't say much. He just sat there and stared at the television, watching game shows. He looks strange without his teeth. Grandmother introduced Dad to the nurse and said he was her brother. Dad just shook his head and looked sad.

We went by their house, and it looked a little better. He had gotten rid of a bunch of junk and said he still had quite a bit of work to do on it. The floors looked nasty and had pee stains all over them from all the cats. Dad said he called someone to come and pick them up. He said that Uncle Justin knew of someone that was interested in the house when it was done. Dad told me he would save some money when he sold the house and buy me a car when I turned sixteen. I told him I wanted a Toyota truck.

Dear Diary,

Ninth grade will soon be over, and then it will be summer. Yippee! If I make it through Biology, it will be a miracle. If it weren't for Tyler helping me study, I would probably fail. My English teacher was the best, and she said that my writing showed promise. She liked my poem I submitted for extra credit. Here it is...

Stepping into the forest path,
I saw the deer run quickly past.
She slowed ahead and turned back to look.
I watched her pause, and then she quickly shook.
She took one step more and looked to the ground.
Her baby lay, sleeping so sound.
I looked with wonder and pure delight,

*To see such a perfect sight.*
*The baby lay so soft and still,*
*And I wondered if it was real.*
*Mama deer looked down and cried.*
*Her baby deer had gone and died.*

*This didn't really happen, but I thought it was kind of cool even though it was sad.*

*Dear Diary,*

*Josie gave me a chicken. She's a Rhode Island Red, and I named her Ruby. She's just a baby right now. She already loves me because I protect her from Linda Lou, the meanest chicken ever.*

*Dear Diary,*

*Tyler's Mamaw has cancer. Tyler and Matt are so bummed. I don't know why. She doesn't even smoke. Gigi and Pops will live forever.*

*Dear Diary,*

*I was at the mall with Tyler today, and I saw R. He grinned at me and then winked. I thought I was going to throw up. Tyler kept asking me what was wrong, and I finally told him I had seen R and that he had winked at me, the slime ball. I wished I had a gun. Sometimes when I think about him, I want to just go to sleep and never wake up.*

*Dear Diary,*

Mom was snooping in my bedroom, but she didn't find my diary. I have it too well hidden. I know that's what she was looking for. She thinks something is wrong with me because I can't pee in public. I don't know why, but if I think someone can hear me, I just can't do it. One day I could, and then boom, I couldn't. The more I think about it, the worse it is.

*Dear Diary,*

Matt, Tyler, and I were at the pool today. Gigi wore her bathing suit, which was really a dress. It came down to her knees. She has big ugly veins all over her legs, and she said they hurt "like the dickens." She bought us all cheeseburgers and fries and told us about when she used to come to the pool all the time with Mom and Josie. Since they don't allow her to smoke anymore, she has to go out to her car to light one up. I told her she needed to quit, but she said I needed to mind my own business.

*Dear Diary,*

Today was the best day ever! Even though he hasn't sold Grandmother and Grandfather Osborne's house, Dad gave me a black Toyota pickup truck for my birthday. It's only a couple of years old, and it's impressive! Tyler is so jealous. He has an old Honda Accord with over 150,000 miles.

# Chapter 13

## *Carly*

Carly was worried about her dad. He was losing weight and looked awful. Once, he had been so handsome but now had dark circles and his hair was thinning. He also had a new girlfriend. Carly didn't see her much because she worked at a bar downtown at night and on most weekends. Her name was Luna, and she had lots of tattoos. Carly didn't share this information with her mom because she knew better now. She knew when to keep her mouth shut.

Her dad was still sweet and loved to see Carly, even though her mom was always hateful to him. If he was one minute late on child support payments, she would act like he was a criminal that needed to go to jail. If Carly tried to defend him, her mother would go crazy, accusing her of being ignorant.

Shelly yelled, "You don't pay the bills, Carly! You have no idea how much I depend on those payments just to make it through each month."

Carly had no idea about bills, but she did know that her dad never complained to her about paying child support. Even though college was a couple of years down the road, her mom was worried he wouldn't have enough money to pay for it. Carly didn't worry about it and said as much to her mom. She didn't know what she wanted to do when she grew up anyway. Shelly said her daughter was going to be college educated and would hopefully be a doctor or lawyer someday. Carly didn't want to be either one. The only thing she was good at was writing, but every time she brought it up, she was told there was no money in that.

Carly and Tyler had both decided to follow Matt to East Tennessee State University in Johnson City. Carly had known that when she went to college, Shelly was supposed to sell the big house. Every time Carly mentioned it to her mom, Shelly told her not to worry about it, that her father wouldn't kick them out. Carly wasn't worried about it, but she *was* worried about her mom, who was more hateful every day. She could tell that her dad had about had it with her mom. Honestly, Carly couldn't blame him for being frustrated about it.

Carly's teachers had praised her writing skills and urged her to keep at it, that she would go far with practice. She had joined the newspaper staff at school at the encouragement of her English teacher. Her favorite subjects were stories that she generated on her own.

Carly's most popular article was about one of the high school janitors. She followed Mr. Dotson around so she could learn as much as she could about his daily jobs. He had talked about his craziest days, which included the time when a bunch of kids had a stomach virus that caused explosive diarrhea. Every bathroom in the school was a mess. He actually became famous after the article was published, and everyone started calling him "Mr. D."

Carly wrote about the ladies in the cafeteria, especially Ms. Lawson, who was everyone's favorite because she would sneak extra ketchup packets if you wanted them. Carly felt bad because Ms. Lawson got in trouble, and the principal told her she couldn't do that anymore.

Carly loved being on the newspaper staff, and her goal was to become the senior editor. Greg Farmer was the current editor. Carly thought he had a big head and a big ego. He had been dating Stacy Brown, who was a cheerleader and one of the most popular girls in the school. Unfortunately, one girl was not enough for him, because he was always flirting. Carly did her best to ignore him.

One day after school, the newspaper staff was discussing ideas for the upcoming Christmas edition. Carly had decided to write about the Christmas parade, which would take place downtown. She had attended parades in the past many times and was looking forward to talking with the people who had entered, especially the car clubs. Her father always entered Grandfather's 1969 Mach 1 Ford Mustang. It was candy apple red with a blacked-out hood, and always a favorite of the parade. He had his construction company decals on the side doors. When Carly was younger, she would ride along with her dad and throw out candy.

While Carly was packing up her things, getting ready to leave, Greg asked if he could talk to her. Carly looked at her watch. It was already getting late, and she was hungry. She put her stuff down and said, "What's up?"

Greg looked amused. "I just wanted to see how you were doing. The parade story will be a great addition to our paper and will probably go on the front page."

Carly was beginning to feel uncomfortable. There was something about the guy that gave her bad vibes. She looked around and noticed that everyone had left but the two of them. She knew her article would be good, but she didn't care where it went in the paper. She did think it deserved to be put on the front, especially with all the lame stories the rest of the staff had come up with.

"Any time you want to sit down and go over anything, I'd be glad to help you. I could help you in any way you need or want," Greg said.

Carly wondered what he was up to. "I appreciate it," she said. "I'll let you know if I need any help."

Greg gave her a perplexing look. "You sure do make this hard."

"What do you mean?" Carly asked.

Greg chuckled. "I mean, I think you're cute, and I'd like to get to know you a little better."

Carly bent down and grabbed her backpack and jacket, mentally trying to figure out how she would respond. "Don't you have a girlfriend?"

Never missing a beat, Greg responded, "Yes, but we're not exclusive. We can see other people whenever we want."

Carly knew that was a lie, but she wasn't going to argue with him. She said, "Thanks, but I don't want to get in the middle of 'whatever' that is."

As she was walking toward the door, Carly said, "Thanks anyway." She was thankful to make her escape, but she was frustrated, wondering if she would have to fend him off the rest of the year.

Unfortunately, the more Carly avoided Greg's advances, the more he pursued her. Obviously, no girl had ever told him no, so Carly figured she was just a novelty and a challenge. By the end of the year, Carly was tired of dealing with him and also sick of the dirty looks Stacy had been sending her way.

Tyler had teased her about it and then got mad when she told him how far Greg had gone. She reluctantly told him about how Greg sent suggestive text messages, telling her what she was missing. He had tricked her into giving him her cell phone number, which she deeply regretted. At first it was friendly, and then became pathetic, alternately begging her for a chance and then accusing her of being a tease.

Everything came to a head at the end of the year newspaper staff party. Ms. Jackson had ordered pizza for the class and gave out awards. Greg also announced the editor's position. The excitement Carly felt about being named Senior Editor for the following year was clouded when Greg began to boast about how he had made it happen. Did he expect a reward in return?

Carly knew she wasn't a tease and had never given him any reason to think she was even remotely interested. At the pizza party, he had cornered her in the hallway when she had gone to the restroom. Seeing him waiting on her as she exited the bathroom door made her stomach drop. Carly froze when he took a step toward her, and then her back was against the wall.

Thinking she was being compliant, Greg began to kiss her, saying, "I knew you wanted it." His hand went behind her neck, pulling her closer.

As soon as Carly felt his tongue, she snapped, jerking her knee up in his groin, causing him to bend over and groan in agonizing pain. For once, he was speechless.

Carly turned to leave and then stopped. "Don't you ever touch me again, or you'll be sorry," she said. Being able to retaliate against Greg was a powerful feeling. She had dreamed of being able to defend herself ever since the humiliation she had felt with River. Back then, she was young and naive with that jerk. With Greg, she knew that she didn't do anything to lead him on in any way. He deserved what she had done to him and more. Next time, she would poke his eyeball out with her pencil, or worse.

# Chapter 14

## Carly

*Dear Diary,*

*Tyler's Mamaw died. He said everything is awful at home. His papaw is getting forgetful like Grandmother and Grandfather. He can't wait to go to college. I'm ready to go too. Mom and Dad are crazier than ever.*

*Dear Diary,*

*I had a date last night. Justin was pretty nice, and he at least didn't try anything. He took me to the Japanese restaurant, and I ate like it was my last meal. It was so good! He'll probably never ask me out again because he won't be able to afford to feed me.*

*Dear Diary,*

*Justin asked me out again! We went on a double date with Tyler and his girlfriend, Erin. We all went to the mall and saw a movie. After we got out, we saw one girl give another girl the middle finger, and then they both started fighting. Next thing you know, a hair weave went flying.*

*Dear Diary,*

Went to see Grandmother and Grandfather Osborne today. Dad had given her a baby doll, and she was holding it when we got there. She gave it to me because she said she was tired of taking care of it. I just hid it in the closet.

*Dear Diary,*

*JUSTIN KISSED ME! IT WASN'T HORRIBLE!*

*Dear Diary,*

Senior year has been good so far. I like being editor, but some of the staff are horrible writers. I practically have to rewrite their articles. Did they not learn anything in English class? Jesse M wrote a story about the student parking lot and said, "Violators will be toad." TOAD!

# Chapter 15

## *Carly*

"Carly! Breakfast is ready!"

Carly rolled out of bed and put her robe and slippers on. It was late January, and there had been a huge snowstorm. The temperatures had plummeted to zero degrees for two nights in a row. The bed had been so warm and cozy, but Carly knew if she didn't go downstairs, her mom would holler again. Nothing got on Carly's nerves more than when her mother hollered, except maybe when she spoke, breathed, or looked at her in that irritating way of hers.

School had been out for three days, and Shelly had closed her shop too. By Saturday, they were both about to go stir crazy. Her mom had cooked everything she had in the house, and they had definitely gained a couple of pounds or more. When she wasn't cooking, her mom was cleaning and organizing, driving Carly up the wall. The electricity had gone out for a few hours the day before, causing them both to have to sit with each other in the dark, a scented candle between them. If Carly had to go through that again, she might as well stick her head in the snow and be done with it.

"It's about time," Shelly said. "Your pancakes are probably cold now."

Carly sat down, poured syrup on her food, and began eating, hoping her mother would stop talking. She hated it when her mother talked when she was trying to eat.

"Did you clean out your closet like I asked you to? I want you to pull out any clothes that you're not wearing so I can take them to the Salvation Army as soon as the roads clear up. Every time I try to hang up something in there, it's a mess."

Carly closed her eyes and chewed slowly.

"Lordy, I don't ask much of you, but if there's anything I hate more, it's when you completely ignore me."

"I'm not ignoring you," Carly said. "I'm just trying to eat my food."

Shelly finally gave up and began washing the dishes. Carly knew it wouldn't last long.

"I want you to give a message to your father," Shelly said.

Carly looked at her mother and wanted to strangle her. She knew how Carly hated to "give messages" to her dad. They were always stupid and hateful.

"You need to tell him that you've decided to go to ETSU," Shelly said. "Now, *he* needs to decide if he's going to apply for a loan, or if he's got some kind of 'hanky panky' money set aside to pay for it."

"Hanky panky money?" Carly rolled her eyes.

"Yes, hanky panky money. I've told you over and over that he's shady, and there's no telling what kind of crooked dealings he's got going on. Sometimes I'm afraid for you to even be around him, and I'll tell you one thing right now. If I could keep you away from him, I would. I'm sure you've seen stuff that you're not telling me." Shelly began wiping the counter furiously. "After all I've done to protect and shield you, I'm always the one that you look at with venom in your eyes. I'm always the bad guy."

Carly groaned inwardly. If she could just make it through the rest of her senior semester, she would never live with her mother again. She would rather live with Gigi and Pops than with her lunatic mother. At least they didn't aggravate her to death.

Yes, she was sure that her dad had his secrets, but her mom had a few secrets of her own. Her best friend in the world, Josie, was going through a depression because her mom had died, and instead of being there for her, Shelly would flirt hopelessly with her husband. Carly had seen it with her own two eyes. She had stopped at Shelly's hair salon after school one day, and there was John sitting in the chair with a cape on. Her own mother was acting like a pathetic teenager. She could tell John was embarrassed too. Good thing he had more sense than to encourage her.

"Don't worry about dad," Carly said. "He's got it all taken care of. He's already been putting money aside."

"Dirty money, I'm sure."

"Would you stop! Dad works hard!"

Shelly threw her rag down. "You think I don't? Do you know how my legs ache after standing on them all day? My lungs are probably full of cancer from all the product fumes I deal with every day. Sometimes I'd like to sit on my butt and do nothing, but I don't have a choice. Just feeding you takes a full-time job."

"You're the one that had to stay in this house," Carly said. "All you had to do was sell it and get a smaller house that you could afford."

"Over my dead body!" Shelly said. "This is my house, and it will be my house until the day I die!"

Carly stood up quickly, her chair sliding across the tile floor, making a loud scraping noise. "You want to know how I feel?" she said. "I hate this house, and I can't wait to get out of here and NEVER come back!"

Carly didn't wait for a response before running out of the kitchen and up to her room. She was too mad to cry. Instead, she grabbed her diary, went into her closet, and shut the door. She wrote, *I HATE HER! I HATE HER! I HATE HER! I HATE HER! I HATE HER!*

Later that day, Carly heard a soft knock on the door. "Carly?"

Carly ignored her.

"Carly, I'm sorry," Shelly said.

Carly sighed. She knew it was coming. Every time they had a big argument, her mom would always come and apologize. At first, it meant something, but now she realized that her mom couldn't be sorry, or she wouldn't provoke her like she did over and over. Why couldn't she just leave her dad alone? Gigi said that Shelly needed to be on nerve pills, or she'd end up in the crazy hospital in Marion where her sister, Sally, went.

Carly had only seen her great aunt Sally one time, and that was enough. She wouldn't stop staring at Carly and told her that if she weren't a good girl, the vultures would carry her to the tower and eat her. Gigi said, "Now, stop that, Sally! Quit being a meanie." Sally just laughed, and even that sounded evil.

Even though she didn't forgive her mother, Carly opened the bedroom door and said, "It's fine. I've already forgotten it."

Carly picked up the bag of clothes she had sorted through and handed them to her mother. "Here's the clothes you wanted," she said. "Can we order pizza for dinner?"

# Chapter 16

## *Shelly*

Shelly carried the clothes downstairs and put them with the rest of the pile she was taking to the Salvation Army. Sometimes, she knew when she was going too far with her daughter, but she just couldn't help herself. She couldn't stop the words from coming out of her mouth. She hated Jared so much, and he brought out the absolute worst in her.

She was worried about Carly. No telling what kind of crazy genes she got from Jared's side of the family. She thought about trying to get Carly into some kind of therapy. If Josie weren't in such a funk, she would call her and ask for advice. Shelly shook her head. Her best friend was so depressed that she didn't have a clue what was going on around her. Since her mom had died, she had just given up on life. Shelly wanted to tell her to snap out of it. If her own mom had died, she wouldn't fall apart. Life has to go on. Poor John was just so sad and didn't know what to do.

Just thinking of John made Shelly smile. She told him to just give Josie time, and if he ever needed anything, she would always be there. She would do anything for that man. If Josie didn't want him, he could always turn to her. She tried to warn Josie that she needed help, but Josie wouldn't listen. John was coming around more. The other day she was trimming his hair, and he looked so despondent that she couldn't help but hug him. For once, he didn't stiffen up but allowed her to hug him, then actually hugged her back.

It wouldn't be Shelly's fault if John turned to her. Josie had no idea that she was pushing John right into her arms. Shelly had waited too long, and since "her John" never appeared, she would take the real thing. Josie would be mad, and Shelly would miss their friendship, but John was worth it.

Shelly pulled out her phone and looked at the texts between her and John. She could just feel it. Soon, John would be hers. Shelly deserved to finally have what she had been hoping and dreaming of for years. It wasn't fair that Josie had John, and she didn't even appreciate him. Josie also had two sons that treated her with respect, not like Carly, who was as hateful as Shelly's mother.

# Chapter 17

## Carly

*Dear Diary,*

*Justin applied and was accepted to a university in Austin, Texas, where his grandparents live. I think we're going to break up. He hinted that he's not good at long distance relationships, like he's ever had one before. Really?*

*Dear Diary,*

*Tyler, Erin, and I went to ETSU last weekend and looked around. We found the first-year dorm rooms. They're old and dingy but I don't care. I can't wait to leave home. I would stay in a tent if I had to. Tyler drove, with Erin in the front seat. I sat in the back seat like a real loser. Every time Tyler and I were talking, she would butt in and talk about something stupid. I wanted to punch her in the face.*

*Dear Diary,*

*Erin's trying to be my best friend now and keeps telling me how much Tyler and her love each other. Makes me want to throw up. I don't want to know the details. We all went to a party, and she kept holding his* hand, not letting him talk to anyone else without her hanging all over him. You could tell it was getting on Tyler's nerves.

Dear Diary,

I think Mom has a boyfriend. She's been on her phone a lot and is very secretive. She's been on a diet too, and now I'm about to starve to death. She won't buy any snacks. I could care less if she has a boyfriend, but if she doesn't quit starving me to death, there's going to be a problem.

Dear Diary,

Graduation was crazy. Everyone came, and when it was over, they all started yelling at each other. Gigi got in trouble with one of the security guards because she lit a cigarette. Pops wore his Tennessee orange colors. Mom and Dad fought because they both wanted to eat lunch with me. I wondered what it would be like if they all got along and were nice to each other. Because Mom was having a special dinner for me that night, I decided to go with Dad, and then Mom got mad at me. Dad also said he wanted to take me to Myrtle Beach. For once, Mom didn't throw a fit. Probably wants to spend more time with her boyfriend.

Dear Diary,

It rained at the beach the whole time we were there. Dad was pretty quiet, like something was on his mind. I tried to get him to talk to me, but he wouldn't. I ate so much seafood that by the time we left, my jeans wouldn't button. I'm going to have to run a marathon now just to fit back into my clothes.

*Dear Diary,*

I haven't even left yet for college, and Mom is already talking about redecorating my room. I don't care because I'm never going back there.

*Dear Diary,*

I'm finally at ETSU! My roommate is from Ohio, and she's kind of lame. She's homesick every day and is such a whiner. I don't miss home one bit. Mom likes to come over and take me out to eat, which is good because I'm getting sick of cafeteria food. She even invites Tyler. It would be better if she weren't so weird.

*Dear Diary,*

Mom is getting crazier by the day. I think Dad is fed up. She still won't sell the house and tells Dad there's nothing he can do about it. I don't know what she's done, but I'm worried about Dad and what he's going to do.

# Chapter 18

## *John*

John sat in his truck and couldn't stop the tears that were falling fast and hard. *What had he done?* That morning when he left the house, he was mad because Josie had rejected him once again. She wouldn't let him get near her, much less touch her. She had given in to her grief since her mom died, and he felt helpless. He wanted to help her, but she wouldn't let him. Last night had been the last straw with her yelling that she might never get over it.

When Shelly had called and asked him to come to the shop and check her dryer vent, he went, even though he knew it was a bad idea. Ever since Josie had become depressed, Shelly had been there for her, as well as himself. At first, she treated him like a friend or brother but gradually she started getting back to the same old Shelly, flirting shamelessly, just like she used to. He knew it was a mistake to let her get by with it. What kind of person does that to her best friend's husband? He was weak and, like a child, needed a little attention.

When Shelly told him she would cut his hair, he let her. When she began hugging him because he was so dejected, he gave in and did what he vowed he would *never* do again. Just like in college, John regretted it immediately.

What was wrong with him? Why was he so weak? Yes, he was mad, but that didn't give him the right to go to Josie's best friend.

John hated himself and prayed Josie would never find out how he had betrayed her.

# Chapter 19

## *Shelly*

"What in the world are you grinnin' about?" Myrtle asked as she looked at Shelly suspiciously through the mirror. "It's rainin' cats and dogs out there, and as soon as I leave here, my money's gonna be wasted."

Myrtle had her hair trimmed the first Saturday of every month. She had been complaining about the weather since she had walked through Shelly's shop. There was nothing she hated worse than when it rained on Saturdays.

"I'm just happy, Myrtle," Shelly said. "Can't I be happy on a rainy day?" Shelly's face heated up just thinking about the night before when John had finally given in to his desires. All those times that she had passed up a doughnut and lived without her nightly potato chips in front of the television had finally paid off. She had lost at least 20 pounds. She had also been walking 10,000 steps a day, even when her legs ached so much she thought she'd die. She was sure John had noticed how much she had improved.

Josie had let herself go, obviously not caring what she looked like. Shelly had seen her at Food City the other day, and her hair was a stringy mess. She could have at least put a comb through her hair and put on a little makeup. John was probably getting pretty tired of her letting herself go like that.

"I don't see how you can be happy when paying customers come in to get their hair done, and it's ruined within minutes of walking out the door," Myrtle said. "I always do my errands after my hair appointment at the beauty shop, and it would be fine and dandy if I could get it all done without a bag over my head."

Myrtle was so cheap; she used a grocery bag to tie around her head when it rained.

"I can't help you anywhere else, but I'd be glad to walk you to your car with the umbrella," Shelly said.

She had to bite her tongue to keep from saying what she really wanted to say, which was, *Quit complaining, you old hag.* She also begged the Lord's help to keep her from strangling Myrtle in front of everyone.

"No, you can't help me." Myrtle sighed deeply to show her aggravation. "Do you know how hard it is to push a buggy and keep the bag from blowin' off my head? You know if it's rainin', the wind's a blowin'."

Shelly took the cape off and brushed the hair from around her neck, all the while rolling her eyes at Jenny in her "help me, please" look.

After her euphoric morning, Shelly was beginning to feel the first irritation of the day. "I'm sorry, Myrtle, but I can't control the weather." Shelly held her hand out for Myrtle so she could help her out of the chair.

Myrtle grumbled all the way to the door, and then to her car, as Shelly held the umbrella for her. "Have a nice day, Ms. Myrtle." *And good riddance!*

As she walked back to the shop door, Shelly's mother pulled in the parking lot. *Oh great! Myrtle and my mother on the same day.* Shelly's mother never showed up with an appointment and always expected free service.

She was hollering before she even got out of the car, "Shelly Francis, I can't do a thing with my hair! I think you may have cut it uneven last time. I need you to straighten it up in the back."

Shelly walked to the door and held it open for her mother. "Jenny, can you check Katy's color?" she asked.

Her mother sat down in the vacant chair without an invitation. Shelly bit her tongue to keep from going off on her mother. "I guess I can probably get it done before I have to rinse Katy out," Shelly said.

There were very few days that Shelly had time to actually take a break or was able to eat sitting down. Someone was always coming in without an appointment, and she rarely turned them down.

Once her mother sat down and she combed her mom's hair, the smoke billowed out, causing Shelly to cough.

Her mom looked at Shelly in the mirror, her wrinkled mouth all puckered up. "I don't want to hear it," she said. "I had a rough morning, and your father is about to drive me batty. I had a few extra smokes, and I needed every one of 'em!"

"What did he do now?" Shelly asked. She didn't know how her mother and father had stayed married for 55 years. They fussed about something every day of their married life.

Once, when she was little, Shelly thought they might get a divorce. Her friend Maddie's parents were getting a divorce, and that got her worried. After a big fight, she cried to her mom, and her mom acted like her daughter was deranged for uttering the word D-I-V-O-R-C-E. "I love your father!" she had said. "Why would you even think such a horrible thing?" From then on, Shelly kept her mouth shut.

"He bought a farm in North Carolina!"

"What?" Shelly shook her head because if there was anything that her father knew nothing about, it was farming.

"He says he can resell it and make money, but how's he going to do that from here?" Shelly's mom asked.

"Good grief. Don't ask me to help. I've got enough to do."

"I wonder if Josie's husband will go and take a look at it. He's a farmer."

Shelly's face colored. As she finished her mom's hair, she looked nonchalant. "I don't know, maybe."

"Well, your father mentioned it, and I said I would ask." Taking her purse from the hook, Shelly's mom said, "You're as red as beet. Are you having hot flashes? Dr. Fleenor has some hormones that will fix you right up." Even though her mother always bragged about not going through "the change," she always acted like she knew everything about it.

Shelly rolled her eyes. "I'm not that old yet!"

"My friend, Nancy, started hot flashin' in her mid-40s," Shelly's mom said. "You're way past that."

"I'm still regular as rain, thank you very much."

"Whoop-di-doo." After digging in her purse for her rain cap, she said, "It's coming, Shelly Francis, whether you like it or not." Shelly couldn't help but stick her tongue out at her mom as she went out the door.

It was definitely coming, and Shelly lied when she said she was as regular as rain. She hadn't been regular for a while, but she refused to accept the fact that she was getting old and always denied having any menopausal symptoms. It was nobody's business.

The rest of the day flew by, and after everyone had left, Shelly sat down in her comfy chair in her breakroom and opened a diet soda. She looked at her phone to see if she had any texts from John about their spectacular night. She was a little disappointed to see that she hadn't heard from him, but he was probably busy with work. She decided to text him to let him know she had been thinking about him.

**Hey, John, hope your day was as wonderful as mine. All I could do was think about you and what we shared last night.**

Actually, it was a very aggravating day. Saturdays usually were when you had Myrtle and Gina on the same day. Besides that, Jared had called again and berated her for her refusal to sell the house. She had given him a piece of her mind, threatening to expose him for all of his dirty deeds. It was all very subtle, but he got the gist of it. She had him right where she wanted him, and there was nothing he could do about it. She would sell when she was ready to sell, and she would get all the profits. He wouldn't receive one dime if she could help it. He didn't want everyone and their brother to know what a pervert he was, or the fact that he was shady with everyone, including the IRS.

Shelly kept looking at her phone to make sure she hadn't missed an incoming text from John. Still nothing. He would definitely text when he was able to; of that she had no doubt.

# Chapter 20

## Carly

Carly was settling into college life, except for the fact that she was worried about her mother. Tyler was worried about his mother too.

"At least your mother isn't acting like a zombie," Tyler said. "Mom looks like she wants to give up and die. She tries to act like nothing is wrong but she's not doing a particularly good job of it."

Carly shook her head. "But my mom is crazier than a loon, and I'm ready to disown her. If I were still a minor, I think I would hire a lawyer and divorce her." Tyler looked skeptical, so she went on, "It's true! I saw it on the news. It's called emancipation of a minor. She just better be glad I didn't know about this sooner."

Carly hadn't even told Tyler the worse part. Her mom had been hinting around that John may divorce Josie and marry her instead. Of all the scenarios, Carly was sure that would be the last thing to happen. Although, she had looked at her mom's phone and saw where she had been texting John. Tyler's dad was as close to perfect as could be. There was no way he would cheat on his wife.

"At least your mom comes over and buys us dinner sometimes," Tyler said. "My mom is too busy moping around to even check on me."

Carly knew that was true, but he had to see how weird her mom was acting, putting on a big show for Tyler, and sometimes Matt if he wasn't working. Carly had been so embarrassed.

They had been studying in the common room of the co-ed dorms, piled up on one of the couches. Carly felt bad for Tyler. He looked so sad when he talked about his mom. As far as Carly was concerned, Josie was the best mom ever, even when she was down in the dumps.

Carly could tell that Tyler wasn't able to concentrate. "Hey, let's go for a walk and clear our heads," she suggested.

Tyler had also been upset about Erin. She had broken up with him and started dating someone else. Once they were on the side-walk, Carly gently punched him in the arm and said, "I'm sorry about Erin."

Carly really wasn't sorry, and it was all she could do to not talk about what a moron she was. Tyler was the best guy she knew. She had always wondered why he never asked her on a date. He did try to kiss her that once but had never tried since.

Tyler turned and walked off the sidewalk and under a shaded tree. The sun was extremely bright, causing the day to be uncomfortably hot.

Carly walked up behind him. "If you want to talk about it, you know I'll always listen," she said. "I'll try my best not to be mean and make fun of her."

Tyler turned around. "I was a little surprised when she broke up with me, but I'm fine, really."

Carly hoped that was true, because Erin wasn't worth it. Carly smiled at Tyler, and Tyler smiled back.

"You know why I'm fine?" he asked.

"Why?"

Tyler took Carly's hand and laced his fingers through hers. "Because... I know you probably don't feel the same way, but it's you that I want to be with, and not just as friends. You have to know that you mean the world to me."

Carly was shocked, and it must have shown on her face.

"Close your mouth, weirdo," Tyler said. "You don't have to say or do anything."

"But I thought...I didn't realize...Really? Are you sure?"

Tyler nodded but didn't say anything else. Carly stood there, stupefied, not knowing what to do. She was in shock.

Finally, Tyler broke the silence. "I'd kiss you, but I don't want you to shove me into the bushes."

Carly laughed. "Last time you did it, I was still thinking about that jerk that painted my room." She looked thoughtful. "I don't think I would do that again."

She wanted to laugh, because all of a sudden, she felt bashful and awkward. This was Tyler, her best friend since they had been babies. They had seen each other naked when they swam in the baby pool together.

Tyler stepped forward, but Carly stopped him by holding up her hand. "Wait a minute," she said. Running her hands through her hair, she began to panic. "We're best friends, Tyler. You mean more to me than anyone else in the entire world, and I don't want to ruin this." Carly pointed at Tyler, and then at herself. "What if we wreck everything and I lose you? I can't even fathom that possibility."

Tyler took Carly's hand and pulled her in for a hug. Carly hugged him back, feeling as if she had come home. Knowing he knew her better than anyone else and wanted to be with her meant everything.

Stepping back, Carly looked up. "You have to know I like you too, Ty."

Tyler started to speak, but she took her finger and placed it on his lips. "Let's take this slow, okay? I need to wrap my head around it. It's a little weird, right? I've looked at you as my best friend forever and now... Wow, this is crazy."

"Just so you know, I've had these feelings for a while now," Tyler said.

Carly looked confused. "But what about Erin?"

"I tried to not think about you that way, so Erin was a diversion. When you and Justin broke up, I thought that we might have a chance. It was now or never, and I didn't want to wait any longer."

Carly looked skeptical. "But Erin broke up with you. You didn't break up with her."

Tyler smiled. "Let's just say I wasn't a good boyfriend, and she got the hint that I was over it. I thought it would be easier for her to break up with me."

"I don't know how you put up with all her whining anyway." It was true. Erin would complain about everything, like if it was too sunny or too cold. The weather never suited her, even if it was perfect. She also ate like a bird, always worrying about gaining weight.

"What about Justin? He was such a tool!" Tyler said.

They both started laughing until Carly said, "Yeah. He was a tool, and I'm glad he went to Texas."

From that moment, Tyler and Carly were inseparable. He was still afraid to kiss her, and she wasn't quite ready for their relationship to go that far. She wanted to assess the waters first but worried he may get impatient. She told Tyler he would know when she was ready.

Carly wanted to tell Tyler about her mom and her obsession with his father, but she was afraid. What if it was nothing? She didn't want to worry Tyler needlessly. There was no way that John would ever leave Josie. He loved her. Carly's mom was just stupid for thinking that he would leave his sweet, beautiful wife for her.

Josie would snap out of her funk eventually, and everything would be fine.

# Chapter 21

## *John*

John heard another notification that he had an incoming text message. He had a sinking feeling that everything was going to explode and life as he knew it would be kaput. Shelly was on a rampage, texting and calling at all hours of the day and night. Thankfully, Josie hadn't noticed since she was still in her slump. He had no idea what to do. He knew better than to think Shelly would forget it and sweep it all under the rug. If he was nice, it only encouraged her to not give up, but if he took a hard stand and told her to stop, there was no telling what she would do. He couldn't let Josie find out.

He hated himself for sleeping with Shelly. It made him sick just thinking of it. He just couldn't understand how he had given in to something so sordid. He knew better, and he also knew how let down everyone would be. Besides Josie, the boys would never understand. Even God was looking down on him with disappointment, which was the worst of all. He knew he wasn't perfect, but he did pride himself in being a good husband and father before all this mess.

At least Josie had enough energy to finally go back to church. He smiled when he thought about how she got mad and left before the service had even started. Everyone was throwing a fit about them sitting in the wrong spot, like they all had assigned seats or something.

Since Josie's mom had died and her ensuing depression, John had been trying to stay out of her way by tinkering in the barn. That's where he was when it all blew up. Shelly had called once again, and he answered just so she would stop. He hoped he could actually get her to see that what they did was a mistake. That night never should have happened. At first, he tried to be nice, and that was when Josie walked into the barn and heard him.

He knew it was over the minute he saw Josie's face. His heart dropped in his chest, and he realized that losing her love would be the worst thing that could ever happen to him.

# Chapter 22

## *Jared*

Jared held the pistol to his head, trying to get up enough courage to shoot himself. If it weren't for Carly, he would have ended it long ago. She was the only good thing in his life. Even though Shelly had done her best to turn his daughter against him, she failed, which had disappointed the heck out of her. He knew he wasn't the best father, but God knew that he loved Carly more than anything, and thankfully she loved him too.

Just thinking about the look in his daughter's eyes when she found out the secrets he tried to keep hidden scared him to death. He didn't want to let Carly down, but it was inevitable. He wished he could change the past, especially when his whole life had shifted. He went from being a happy and normal 12-year-old boy to being scared, mistrustful, and wretched.

Mr. Owens had been their neighbor for as long as Jared could remember. He had a dune buggy that he drove on special occasions. You could hear it all over the neighborhood once he started it up. When the kids heard the telltale sounds of the rumbling engine, they would all begin running toward his house because he would take as many as he could fit in the vehicle to the market, where he would buy them all candy and treats. Back then, they didn't even worry about seatbelts, and they would oftentimes pack themselves in like sardines.

Jared and his brother, Justin, felt privileged because they lived next door to Mr. and Mrs. Owens. They would often invite them in for cookies, cake, and ice cream. Mrs. Owens always kept their favorite sodas in the refrigerator too. The best part was their dog. They had a basset hound named Oliver, and he was the best dog ever. He loved to play with the boys and also enjoyed the extra attention.

The day things changed forever started out like any other day. Justin had a cold, so he stayed home that Saturday. Jared was bored and decided that he wanted to play fetch with Oliver. His mom had let them buy a new toy for the dog, and he couldn't wait to show it to him. Mrs. Owens wasn't there because she was visiting her sister in Knoxville. Mr. Owens invited him in anyway and gave him a candy bar, one of Jared's favorites. He told him that it was too hot for Oliver to play fetch outside, so they would just watch television instead. He was watching a movie and wanted Jared to watch it with him.

Jared thought it was a pretty stupid movie, but then something happened that caught his attention. Next thing he knew, the men in the movie were taking their clothes off and doing things that stunned Jared. Mr. Owens was acting like it was nothing, but Jared couldn't take his eyes away. He hadn't even noticed when Mr. Owens was right next to him, and when he did finally realize it, Mr. Owens began touching him. Once again, Jared was in shock and couldn't stop him. What happened next would change him forever.

Mr. Owens told him later never to tell anyone what had happened. He said it was normal, but it was nobody's business. Jared didn't want to tell anyone. He was embarrassed and mortified, but the worst part was that he couldn't forget it. No matter how hard he tried over the years, it was there in his mind. When he got older, it got worse.

He knew he wasn't a homosexual, but there was something that kept drawing him back, something he would never understand. He married

Shelly because he loved her, although it became clear soon enough that she loved someone else. John didn't reciprocate those feelings, he was sure, but knowing Shelly longed for her best friend's husband was degrading and brought Jared's self-esteem low.

Poor Josie didn't have a clue. Shelly told him that she was John's first and that it happened when he was in college, and also that Josie didn't know. Jared tried his best with Shelly, but it was never enough, and he knew it never would be because of her obsession with John.

Shelly had finally returned his call. After Jared told her that he had contacted a realtor and that there would be no more delays in selling the house, she began ranting and raving, and when that didn't seem to work, she resorted to threatening. She threatened to expose him to everyone, especially Carly. She said Carly deserved to know the worthless piece of trash her father was. She also said she would call the IRS as soon as they opened the next day.

Jared put his gun down and looked at pictures of Carly on his phone. His baby girl was his pride and joy. He wiped away the tears that spilled on his phone. He thought about Shelly and all the threats over the years that had caused him to be miserable and depressed for so long.

He picked the gun up again and played with the safety. He knew where to aim so that he would never suffer, and he would die immediately. Every time he was ready to pull the trigger, he would think of his daughter again. In the end, he just couldn't do it. He couldn't kill himself, but somehow, he had to stop Shelly.

# Chapter 23

## *Carly*

Carly and Tyler had finished their first year at ETSU. The last semester was a little more difficult than the first, but she made it, and her grades weren't too bad. Her GPA was a little higher than Tyler's, not that it was a competition or anything. Carly's parents were still at war, but that was nothing new. Her mom was a little more agitated than usual too, but that was nothing new either. Gigi said she was going through the change, and that made older women crazy. She said she never went through it herself.

Tyler had moved into his brother Matt's apartment after school was out, while Carly found a room to rent in an older couple's house. Thankfully, Gigi and Pops agreed to help out with the costs. Knowing she didn't have to move back home for the summer was a relief.

Mr. and Mrs. Holloway always rented a room to a college student. Carly had found out from one of her professors that the room had just become available, and with her recommendation, Carly was able to secure it quickly. The room was located in their basement, which had its own private entrance. It was perfect with basic furniture to fit all of her needs. She also had her own private bathroom.

The Holloways were a little strange, but Carly figured it was because they were from Canada. She had never met anyone from Canada before. They were both retired professors and liked to work in their garden all day, where they grew their own vegetables and herbs. They had a large following on social media, called "The Holistic Holloways." They knew the purpose of every weed, whether it was medicinal or provided well-being. They didn't believe in over-the-counter meds, preferring a natural remedy instead.

Carly fit right in because she was quiet and didn't have any friends come over except for Tyler. One time when Carly had a cold, Margie (Mrs. Holloway) gave her ginger tea and an onion poultice to sleep with on her feet. Carly was skeptical but went with it. She couldn't believe how much better she felt the next day. It was great, except for the fact that her room and feet smelled like onions.

Carly and Tyler hadn't told their parents that they were dating yet, not that much of anything had happened. They often held hands, and Tyler would sometimes kiss her on the forehead. She had to laugh when thinking of the frustration on his face. Sometimes he felt like the best friend that she had known her whole life, and then sometimes she wanted to cry because her emotions would be overwhelming. She wanted to grab him and kiss him until they both couldn't breathe.

Of course, Matt knew about them dating. He didn't seem surprised and treated her like he always had, like a sister. Every time Carly and Tyler got to know Matt's girlfriends, he would get tired of them and move on. Sometimes they would double date, and sometimes, the three of them would hang out, just like old times.

Tyler told her that he was going to follow his brother in a law enforcement career. He had gotten a job working security at the mall. Carly was working part-time as a barista at a coffee café downtown. She loved Johnson City and didn't plan on ever moving back to Bristol. She only wished it was farther away from her mother.

Carly looked at her phone. She had been texting Tyler about their date. He was going to pick her up and take her to see a movie that had just been released. She stopped at the store earlier and bought a bunch of candy, including chocolate peanut butter cups, his favorite.

It was a romantic comedy, which should be interesting, since they usually watched science fiction or fantasy-adventure films. Maybe tonight would be the turning point in their relationship.

# Chapter 24

## *Shelly*

Shelly saw Josie enter the shop out of the corner of her eye but continued to talk to her client as if she hadn't seen her. Peeking at her in the mirror, the look on Josie's face was clear. So, now Josie knew the truth. Instead of being ashamed, Shelly was glad. She was glad Josie finally knew the reality of the situation. Josie could get on with her life without John. He would be able to leave her and come live with Shelly at last. She glanced around to see her customers become alert, especially Myrtle, who was waiting to get her hair washed.

Shelly finally gave in and looked at her best friend. She was surprised at the haggard look on Josie's face and felt just a moment of remorse. "I wasn't expecting you, Josie," Shelly said.

Before Josie could begin making a scene in front of all her customers, Shelly told her to come to the back room so they could talk in private. She had decided that it wasn't the time to admit to their affair, especially at her place of business, and played as if Josie was being senseless.

Josie wasn't having it, though, and tried in every way to make Shelly feel unscrupulous, as if loving John was sordid. Josie was the one who pushed John away. She didn't want him anymore, and the Lord knew that Shelly wanted him, now and for always. Shelly didn't want to lose her best friend, but for John, she would give everyone up just to be with him. Carly didn't need Shelly anymore and acted like she hated her.

Shelly had already resigned herself to this confrontation. It had to happen eventually because it was inevitable, but she wished it wasn't at the salon. Josie, looking certifiably insane, yelled and threatened her so that everyone in the whole salon had to hear. Most of them knew her best friend, but hopefully they wouldn't judge Shelly too much. They didn't know the whole story and that Josie had practically pushed John into her arms. They didn't know how much Shelly loved John or how perfect they would be together. She let Josie get it all out of her system until the rant was finally over, and then Shelly asked her to leave before she began yelling again. There was nothing Josie could say that would make her feel sorry for what she had done.

It was over. Done. Friendship ended. Now, they could all move forward. Who needed friends when you had the perfect man.

# Chapter 25

## Carly

*Dear Diary,*

    *The movie was awesome, but the kiss afterwards was even better. When the credits began rolling, I looked at Tyler and he looked at me. That was it. Now, we can't stop kissing.*

*Dear Diary,*

    *Mom is certifiably insane. She is obsessed with John, and I told her that if she didn't stop, it would be the death of her. Why can't she act like a normal person?*

*Dear Diary,*

    *Tyler said things are weird with his mom and dad. I'm so worried, but I know that it's my mom's fault. I should have told him a long time ago, and now I don't know what to do.*

*Dear Diary,*

    *If it weren't for Tyler, I don't know what I would do. Besides Mom acting like a nut job, Dad is acting funny too. Yesterday, he told me that no matter what happens, he loves me. What is he talking about? What is going to happen? I can't take this anymore.*

*Dear Diary,*

    *Gigi said Pops had another mild heart attack, but he's okay now. She was crying and said she didn't know what she would do without him. Mom acted like she didn't even care. Pops called me and told me not to worry, that he was fine.*

# Chapter 26

## *Shelly*

Shelly couldn't believe it! She had finally called John at home out of desperation because he wouldn't answer or return her calls on his cell phone. She tried to get through to him, but Josie got on the line and said she and John were back together and to leave him alone. As if Shelly could just turn off her feelings for the man she loved most in the world.

She had been so mad and hurt that she blurted out to Josie that she had been John's first. She could tell that Josie was shocked, but she had to know. She had to know that John loved her too and that what they shared was special. Josie only wanted him back because she was jealous.

After Josie was silent, John got on the phone and said terrible things to Shelly. She knew he didn't mean it when he said he would get a restraining order against her. He said he didn't love her, but she knew that was a lie too. That night at the shop proved it. John would never be able to forget her. Their love had laid dormant for a while, but it was alive now, their passion strong and real.

Josie didn't love John like Shelly did. All she cared about were her boys and her mother. She never put John first. Once John left Josie and came to her, she would always put him first. He would realize what real love was once she poured her heart and soul into their relationship.

Shelly decided to back off and give John time to end things with Josie. She needed to check on her father anyway. He'd had a mild heart attack, and her mother acted like he was dying, like she cared. For Shelly's whole life, her mom had complained about what a slob her dad was and how he got on her nerves. Shelly bet that her mom was planning his whole funeral, just in case.

Shelly tried to give John space, but it didn't last long because she just couldn't stay away. John consumed her thoughts. Every waking moment, he was on her mind and even in her dreams. Sometimes her dreams with John were lovely, but sometimes they were disturbing, like the ones with the blood. The first time she dreamed it, it had caused her to wake up in a panic remembering the blood on her hands that she couldn't wash off. She had to be careful, or she would end up like her Aunt Sally. Her mom would gladly throw her into the mental hospital, just like she did her sister.

Any time Shelly was out, she would drive by John's work to see if she could catch him there, and it finally happened. He was in the parking lot, and Shelly knew it was fate. But instead of being glad to see her, he was mad. She couldn't understand it. He even threatened, again, to take out a restraining order against her. Why would he do that? He knew she loved him more than anything in the whole wide world. It had to be Josie. She was turning him against her. Shelly knew she couldn't let that happen.

Shelly remembered the day Josie came to her shop and confronted her. There had to be legal ramifications for Josie coming in and disrupting her business. How would Josie feel if she got a restraining order against her? Did John know what she had done, yelling so loud that everyone could hear about their personal business? John would be crushed! It was time that he saw what kind of person she really was. It was time for payback, and Josie would get hers.

Shelly knew exactly what to do because of the time she put a restraining order on that lunatic, Miranda Thompson. Miranda had accused

Shelly of trying to steal her husband, as if Shelly would have been so desperate. Sure, Joey was a looker and especially a flirt, but she didn't want him. He was a little diversion at one time, but nothing serious and definitely not husband material. Someone—and it had to be that hideous Miranda—spraypainted obscene messages all over the front of the shop. Getting the restraining order and threatening to sue them both stopped all the threats.

Shelly would just love to see the look on Josie's face when she was served with her own restraining order.

# Chapter 27

## Jared

Jared used his old key to let himself inside his old house. Of course, Shelly wasn't smart enough to change the locks.

He wasn't sure what he was going to do, but he did know that he had to confront Shelly and tell her that things had to change. He was going to do a little threatening of his own. Did Josie know of Shelly's obsession with John and that it had been going on as long as he could remember?

Jared didn't want to hurt Josie and John, but he had no choice. If word got out about his private life, his business would be ruined and his life over. Besides, his parents were racking up tons of debt in that nursing home, and he needed cash. He hadn't realized how terrible things had gotten until he looked into their finances.

His mom had been spending all their money on online shopping, and the worst part was that it was on things they didn't even need. He had always thought because of their hoarding tendencies that they never threw anything away, and that's why they had so much stuff. He found out that she had spent their retirement and maxed out all of their credit cards on nothing but junk. It was an addiction, and she couldn't stop. With her dementia, things had gotten so out of hand that you couldn't walk through the house for all the unopened boxes. His father was clueless. His dementia had progressed so fast that he was non-verbal.

The house was so bad that it took all he had to complete the updates and repairs. It took forever to sell, and he didn't get the profit he was counting on because of the neighborhood, which had gone downhill. Their next-door neighbor was a part-time mechanic and always had a car in the driveway in the middle of an overhaul. He couldn't even look at the Owen's house, even though they were long gone. Many buyers wouldn't even look at the house after seeing the messy and disorderly street. He had to take a ridiculous offer just to get it off of his hands. By the time he split the profits with Justin, it wasn't worth all the time and effort he put into it.

Jared looked around the house he built for Shelly, trying to assess its re-sell value. It needed updating too, but if there was one good thing about Shelly, it was her housecleaning skills. Most people wanted to update to their own tastes anyway. The house was immaculate, which was a plus in the market. The open staircase was a waste of space, but buyers would be impressed as they walked in the front door. The neighborhood was still popular and convenient to town. Being outside the city had advantages too, like lower taxes.

Jared went to their old bedroom and sat in one of the window seats. He had put a lot of money and sweat into the house, and it was top of the line in craftmanship. He noticed that Shelly still loved the color purple. The bedroom wasn't gaudy but in soft, muted shades of lavender with accents of white.

Their past wasn't all bad. Memories of happier times made Jared smile. He loved it when Carly would crawl in their bed at night and snuggle in between them. When she was about five years old, he had taught her to ride her bike up and down the neighborhood sidewalk. She loved to play soccer in the backyard and basketball in the driveway, which irritated Shelly to no end.

He had tried with Shelly, but nothing was ever good enough. He worked so hard to provide for his family, and even that backfired because he would be working on the jobsite instead of being with her at home. He couldn't win, and then when she found out about Greg, it was over. She never looked at him the same way again and, really, he couldn't blame her. It was his deepest, darkest secret.

Just when he thought he could put the past behind him, something would trigger his disgusting need. He had prayed to God, but he couldn't stop. Greg was married and also hid his darker side from the world. They would both stay away from each other as long as they could, until they couldn't. It was a vicious cycle and he hated it.

As he sat there remembering and lamenting, it had grown darker. He saw headlights flash through the window. Shelly would have a cow when she saw his truck. He parked it so that it was well hidden from the street view, but Shelly saw it. She was yelling as soon as she walked in the door, but Jared kept quiet in the darkened bedroom. Eventually, she made it upstairs and came storming through the door and found him.

"How dare you!?" his ex-wife fumed. "What are you doing in *my* house?"

Jared sat there quietly until Shelly stopped yelling and pulled out her cell phone. "You've got about ten seconds, and then I'm calling the police," she said.

"I wouldn't do that if I were you," Jared said.

"Are you kidding me? You are trespassing, and they'll throw your butt in jail."

"I don't think so," Jared said. "My name is on the deed to this house. Since you have blatantly ignored the terms of our divorce settlement, I have every right to come here and kick *your* butt to the curb." Jared wasn't exactly sure what his rights were, but it sounded about right to him, and he could tell by the look on Shelly's face, she wasn't sure either.

Steam began billowing off the top of her head as she said, "Get out of this house, Jared, or I'll tell everyone who will listen what a fraud you are. I'm telling them of your secret homosexual affairs. I've already turned you into the IRS. You'll be a laughingstock in this town." She threw her purse down in frustration. "I mean it, Jared. I'm not fooling around. Now, get out."

"I don't think so," Jared replied.

Shelly stared at Jared in disbelief.

"What about your own little secrets, Shelly?" he asked. "Huh? You want it to get around that you have the hots for your best friend's husband? What will Josie think about that?"

Shelly's mouth was open, but instead of getting angrier, she began laughing. "That's all you've got? You're going to have to come up with something better than that."

The look of confusion must have been on Jared's face, because she began to elaborate. Stepping closer, Shelly got in his face and said, "They already know. It's only a matter of time until John leaves Josie and comes to live with me, here in this big ole house that you're going to pay for. Got it?"

Jared closed his eyes and knew that he had lost the game. His trump card was nothing but a deuce. Except that Jared wasn't going to lose this time. Not by a long shot. He stood up, as if defeated, and walked toward the doorway.

"That's right," Shelly said. "Get out and don't ever darken my doorway again. Just pay the bills, and we'll get along fine. Carly won't have to find out what a loser father she has."

Jared stopped and knew that Shelly was right behind him. She never knew when to quit, but this time would be the last. Jared had a wrench in his pocket, and he gently pulled it out. As if in slow motion, he swung the wrench and hit Shelly on her forehead, knocking her out instantly and stopping her tirade. He could only think of the blessed peace her silence offered.

The blood began pooling around Shelly's head at an alarming rate, and Jared knew she must be dead. He felt her wrist for a pulse. Nothing. She was dead in one blow.

Jared wasn't sorry. Shelly had made his life a living hell for so long. God forgive him, but he was glad she was dead. Jared calmly walked out of the house and drove home.

# Chapter 28

## Carly

Carly was at the coffee house working when her grandmother called. "Honey, I've got some shocking news," she said. "I need you to sit down."

Carly knew it must be pretty important if her grandmother called her. She hated to talk on the phone and usually sent short texts when she needed to communicate.

"Hold on," Carly said. "I'm at work, and I need to make sure someone can cover for me."

Carly walked to her manager's office and asked her if she could take an important phone call. She thought the world of Lisa, not only because she hired her the day she met Carly, but because she was fun and supportive. She allowed Carly to be creative in the shop and appreciated her diligence and dedication at work.

Carly walked back to their small lounge room and sat on the old leather couch. "What's up, Gigi?" she said.

Carly was alarmed when she heard her grandmother let out a sob. "It's your mother, Carly. She's...She's been murdered."

Carly shook her head because she knew that she must not have heard her grandmother correctly. She couldn't have just said that her mother was murdered. Why would Gigi say something like that?

"Carly, did you hear me?"

"I heard you, and I don't believe you," Carly said.

"It's true, hon," Gigi said. "I'm so sorry. I'm not good at things like this. Can someone bring you home? I don't want you to drive."

"You just said someone murdered Mom," Carly said. "What...I don't... It's not true, is it, Gigi? Please tell me it's not true!"

For the first time in her life, Carly heard her grandmother crying. Her grandfather got on the line.

"Punkin', I know it's awful," Pops said. "We don't know much, but when Shelly didn't come in to work or answer Jenny's call, she went to her house. She found her. Your mom is gone. Have someone drive you to our house, and we'll try to get through this."

Carly couldn't say anything and disconnected the phone. She was in shock and couldn't think of what she should do or think. What did a person do when they found out their mother had been murdered? It didn't seem right to do anything, so Carly just sat there until Lisa came back to check on her.

Lisa must have seen the look of utter shock on Carly's face because she immediately came and sat next to her and took her hand. "What is it, Carly?" she asked. "What's wrong?"

Carly looked at her boss and tried to speak, but great, huge sobs escaped out of her mouth. Lisa pulled Carly close and tried to console her.

"It's okay, Carly. Just let it out."

Lisa comforted Carly until she heard the bell ring in the café. She grabbed a throw blanket and wrapped it around her shoulders. "Let me take care of this customer, then I'm going to close the café," she said.

Carly nodded, and Lisa left the room. Once she was by herself, she pulled the blanket tighter. It smelled of coffee, which comforted her. Her mom loved coffee. She was very particular and snubbed her nose at the store brands and preferred ordering her beans and grinding them herself every morning. Carly had also come to love the fresh smells and would sometimes bring her mom gourmet brands that the café sold. Shelly would get so excited.

Her mother was gone now. Carly couldn't wrap her mind around it. It just seemed too unbelievable and bizarre. The last time she had talked to her mother, they had a fight, which wasn't unusual. The conversation started off good, but then Shelly started ranting and raving about her dad again. Carly yelled at her mom and said she didn't want to hear it and hung up on her. Now, she would never hear her voice again. Carly didn't want that! She wanted to have a good relationship with her and to not fight about her dad. Why couldn't she leave it alone? Why did she always have to ruin everything? Carly stood up and threw the blanket down. She was pacing when Lisa walked back into the room.

Carly stopped. "My mom's dead. Someone murdered her!"

Lisa placed her hand on her chest. "Oh my...Carly! I'm so deeply sorry!"

Carly put her hands in the air. "I hated her!"

Lisa shook her head. "You didn't hate her, Carly. You were frustrated with her, but you never hated her."

Carly shook her head. Lisa reminded her of Josie. She was kind and always saw the good in others. Lisa had invited her to church so many times, but Carly always found an excuse not to attend. She knew she wasn't good enough to go to church and would only sit there like a hypocrite. They didn't see the horrible person she really was. God said you were supposed to love everyone as He loved you. There were very few people that Carly loved or respected. She wished she could be better. She wished she could be more understanding. She wished she could have seen the good in her mother and not just the bad. Now, it was too late for anything. Her mom died thinking that Carly hated her.

"But I did hate her," Carly said and sat down again, sobbing her heart out. "I hated her so much...but I wanted to love her." Great sobs tore from her soul. Now that she was crying, she couldn't stop.

Lisa grabbed tissues from her desk and gave them to Carly, taking one for herself. "Sweetheart," she said, "it's okay to have those feelings of frustration with your parents."

Carly had already confided to Lisa the contentious relationship she had with her mother and father. Lisa tried to tell her that it was normal and that her mother would eventually stop trying to pull Carly between her parents, and if she didn't that Carly would have to learn how to stop it herself. She said Carly had to be firm and refuse to be dragged into whatever quarrel was prevalent at the time. That's why Carly hung up on her mother, but instead of doing it calmly, Carly had screamed and yelled and then hung up, refusing to take any more calls or texts. It had been at least three days since her mom tried to contact her.

Lisa patted Carly's back. "The worst thing you can do is feel guilty about actions or feelings right now," she said. "Your mom had to know on some level that she was pushing you and goading you. We're all human, and we do and say things that we regret later, but we just can't help ourselves. You need to think about the good times right now. It's going to be the hardest thing you've ever done, but God will take care of you. He will give you the strength to push through. Let your family and friends be there for you. Please don't push them away. Can I say a prayer with you right now?"

Carly nodded, not sure what good it would do. She guessed, at least, it couldn't hurt. Why would God do anything for her, anyway? She didn't deserve it. She listened to Lisa's prayer half-heartedly and wondered how she was going to survive.

Lisa offered to take Carly to her grandparents, but she declined and called Tyler, who was on his way to the mall to start his shift. When he answered, she began crying and couldn't speak. Lisa took the phone and walked away from the breakroom. She told him what was going on and that Carly was in bad shape.

"I'm on my way," Tyler said. "I'll be there in five minutes."

Tyler ran into the café and pulled Carly into his arms, holding her and petting her, giving her time to calm down.

Speaking into Tyler's chest, Carly murmured, "She's dead, Tyler. Someone murdered my mom."

"Who?" he asked.

"I don't know," Carly said. "Gigi called. She said they didn't know anything but to go to their house. Maybe I'll find out something. Can you take me?" She looked at Tyler with eyes already red and swollen. "I don't think I can drive."

More sobs arose from her body. Would she ever stop crying?

"Of course," he said. "Let me call work and let them know."

On their way back to Bristol, Carly called her dad and told him the news.

"Oh, sweetie, I'm so sorry," he said. "What can I do?"

Carly cried and told him that she would call him later, that she needed to see her grandparents to find out everything she could.

Once they pulled in the driveway, Carly's grandfather was at the front door, holding it open. He looked as if he had aged 10 years since Carly had last seen him. They walked into the house and found Gigi on the couch smoking.

"Oh, Carly, your poor mother is dead!" Gigi said. "Someone knocked her on the head and left her. Blood was everywhere!"

Carly began crying softly and sat next to her grandmother, unsure if she should hug her or not. The ashtray on the coffee table held a pile of cigarettes, and smoke drifted in great clouds in the room. Not receiving any encouragement, Carly sat still, keeping her arms to herself.

"Frank, tell them what that officer said," Gigi said.

"Gina, I don't think Carly needs to hear that."

Tyler sat next to Carly on the couch and took her hand, rubbing it softly. She thanked him with her eyes, showing her gratitude.

Her grandmother lit another cigarette and turned her head away from Carly, blowing smoke out of her mouth. "They think it was somebody she knew because there was no break-in," Gigi said. Waving her hand in the air to dissipate the smoke, she continued, "Who would do that? Do you know of anyone that she's been fighting with lately? Remember that girl who sprayed those hateful things at the beauty shop? Shelly might have been sleeping with someone else's man, and they killed her for it. I loved my Shelly, but she didn't always make the best decisions."

Carly's grandfather shook his head. "Would you for once in your life stop talking?" he asked. "Your daughter hasn't been dead twenty-four hours, and you're already bad-mouthing her."

"Shut up, Frank! I wasn't bad-mouthing her. I was just telling the truth. You got any bright ideas?"

"It could have been a burglar!"

Carly squeezed Tyler's hand and then stood up. "I think...I think I need to go to the house," she said.

Carly's grandfather shook his head. "You can't do that, darlin.' It's a crime scene, and they've got everything quartered up. They've promised to find out who did this, and we've got to let them do their job."

Carly nodded. "Okay," she said. "I just need some air." As Tyler followed her to the door, Carly told her grandparents, "I may be back later, I'm not sure."

Her grandmother stood up. "Try not to think bad of your mother, Carly," she said. "She had her faults, but she loved you. I tried my best with Shelly, and nothing I did ever made her happy. She just couldn't be satisfied, always wanting more. I told her that marrying Jared was the best thing she ever did. He was a good father, and he made a good living. I don't know why she hated him like she did. I told her just the other day—"

But Carly couldn't take any more. "I've got to go, Gigi," she interrupted. "I'm sorry, I just can't right now."

"Now, see what you've done?" Carly's grandfather said. He took his hat off and brushed his leg with it.

The last words Carly heard were, "Shut up, Frank!"

Carly told Tyler to drive by her house. Tyler said, "I don't think it's a good idea, Carly."

"Please, just do it," she said. "We don't have to stop, but I want to see what's going on."

Tyler sighed and drove in the direction of the house. They were there within five minutes, but the road was blocked, and they couldn't go any farther. Once the car stopped, Carly jumped out and ran as close as she could to the house until an officer forcibly stopped her.

Carly yelled, "That's my house!"

"I'm sorry, honey, but you can't go any farther," he said. "There's an investigation going on."

"But my mom is dead, and I need to find out what's going on," Carly said. By that time, Tyler had parked the car and was by her side with his arm around her.

"Let me take down your information," the officer said. "I'm sure the investigators will want to talk to you."

"Carly!"

Carly looked around and saw her father running toward her.

"Daddy!"

Carly ran to her father, and they both held each other tightly. "Daddy, what are we going to do?" she asked.

"It's okay," he said. "It will all be okay."

"No, it won't. Somebody murdered Mom!" Carly wiped her eyes. "Someone was in her house and hit her on the head."

Her dad looked distressed. "Do you know who...did this?"

The officer patiently explained that the investigation was underway and took down her father's information, as well as Carly's. She knew she wasn't getting anywhere, so she finally relented and left the premises. Carly sent Tyler home and went with her dad.

They stopped at her grandparents for a little while, then went to his house. They were both in shock, but Carly was glad to be with her dad because, like Tyler, she knew that he would be there for her. She promised Tyler that she would call him the next day.

# Chapter 29

## *Jared*

Seeing his little girl's overwhelming grief was just about more than he could take. Jared had been glad that Shelly was dead—that was, until he came back to his senses. How could he have killed someone, especially his daughter's mother? What had he done? He didn't mean to kill her, but something inside him just snapped.

He held Carly and tried to comfort her the best that he could. She would always be his little, precious girl. He loved her more than anyone, ever since she came into the world screaming her head off. She had been almost purple, causing Jared, Shelly, and even the hospital staff to be alarmed. She didn't like the traumatic effects of birth, and she wanted everyone to know about it. Once she calmed down, Carly stared intently at him with those dark eyes that would eventually become the brightest blue. Her hair was almost black and at least an inch long all over her tiny head.

The nurse told them that it would fall out, but it never did. By the time she was a year old, Shelly had been putting it up in ponytails. Shelly always claimed that Carly was just like her, but Gina said that Shelly had been baldheaded until she was at least two years old.

Jared wanted so much for his little girl, and he wanted to always be there for her, but Shelly was always pushing him out of the way. Even when they were married, she complained when he didn't work enough, and then she complained when he worked too much, saying he was never there for them.

By the time they divorced, he wasn't quite sure what to do with his daughter, but Carly didn't seem to mind. She was always glad to be with him, even if it was just going out to eat and getting a movie or video game, which were the only things he knew to do at the time. That was why he never got mad if she tried to get his attention when he was on the phone. How could you get mad at someone who wanted to spend time with you?

Jared went to his bedroom and checked on Carly. She was finally able to go to sleep. They stayed up talking, and when it was past midnight, he told her to lie down in his bed. He would gladly sleep on the couch if he thought he could actually sleep.

What was Carly going to do when she found out the truth? Jared knew he would lose her forever. He hadn't wanted to go to the house earlier that day, but wouldn't it look odd if he didn't? He tried to act normal, but he was shaking so hard, scared that everyone could see right through him.

A friend of his who worked at the police station confided to him that the investigation was focusing on John Carrier, Josie's husband. Shelly had placed a restraining order against her best friend, then Shelly had confronted John in the parking lot at his job, causing a scene.

Jared didn't know how to feel. He didn't want John to go down for a murder he didn't commit, but Jared couldn't confess either. He went into the bathroom and found the meds he needed to take the pain away. He needed sleep, and he also needed something to make him forget.

# Chapter 30

## *Carly*

Carly woke up the next day and found her dad asleep on the couch. She went into the kitchen and found coffee in one of the cabinets. After making a pot, she looked around to see if she could find anything to eat, not that she was very hungry. After finding out-of-date bacon, she grabbed her father's keys and decided to go to a drive-thru for breakfast.

Her dad was still on the couch when she returned. She poured coffee, ate her biscuit, and called her grandparents, who hadn't heard anything from the investigators. Two hours later, her dad was still asleep. She began making loud, intentional noises just so he would wake up, but to no avail. Finally, she began shaking him, but he only groaned and didn't open his eyes. Worried, Carly put a cold rag on his face, and when that didn't work, she splashed water on him.

"Wake up, Dad!" Carly yelled.

Jared opened his eyes and blew water out of his mouth. "What are you doing?" he asked.

"Trying to wake you up," Carly said. "You sleep like the dead!"

Her father smacked his lips and made a face.

Carly nodded and said, "Yes, and your breath smells awful. Are you okay?" She picked up her dad's phone and handed it to him. "Your phone keeps dinging. It's an unknown number. It may be the investigator."

Her father slowly sat up and tried to focus his eyes on his phone, but it was blurry. Carly grabbed it out of his hands. "Let me," she said. "What is your password?" She wondered if he took something. "Did you take something to make you sleep?"

"Yes, sorry," Jared said. "I must have taken it too late."

Carly could understand that. She had a tough time falling asleep too. "You have a voicemail from Detective Fuller," she said. "He wants you to call him asap."

Carly handed him the phone.

"Let me make coffee first so I can wake up," Jared said.

"I made some already, but it's a couple of hours old," Carly said. "Want me to make a fresh pot? I also went to Bojangles and got breakfast."

Her dad shook his head. "No, it's fine." He poured a cup, drinking it black. "You okay this morning?"

Carly sighed. "As well as I can be, I guess. I think I'm through crying." Carly's eyes were still swollen, even after she had kept ice on them. "I still can't believe it."

They both sat in silence, contemplating the past 24 hours. Her dad walked to the paper bag sitting on the kitchen counter. He took a bite of his biscuit and wrapped it back up. "Sorry, babe, I don't think I can eat anything," he said.

"It's okay. I just wanted to do something so I would quit thinking about Mom and her lying in her room all bloody."

"Carly, please don't," Jared said.

Carly put her hand over her mouth and hung her head. "I can't help it, Daddy!" She felt her dad wrap his arms around her shoulders. "I just keep thinking about her lying there with blood everywhere. She would have had a fit knowing blood was all over the carpet."

"I'm so sorry, sweetie," he said. "I wish...I wish I could make it better."

Carly turned to her father. "Just having you with me means every-thing, Daddy."

Carly couldn't help but notice how sad her dad was. After the way her mother had treated him for so many years, he still had love and compassion for her.

Jared cleared his throat. "Let me call the detective and see what he needs."

Carly busied herself in the kitchen, all the while eavesdropping on her father's conversation. When he finally hung up, she asked him, "Well, what did he say?"

"He wants us both to come down to the station, but he said it shouldn't take long," he said. "They just need to iron out details for the investigation. Do you want me to take you back to Johnson City to get your car later?"

"No. I've been texting with Tyler. He and his brother Matt are going to the farm to see Josie and John. He said he would pick me up after that."

"Okay. We need to leave here in about an hour, so I'm going to jump in the shower."

While her dad cleaned up, Carly walked the floors, trying to think of everything but her mom. She pulled out her phone and began scrolling through social media. She had several notifications, which were unusual since she didn't post much, the last thing being a picture of some latte art with a swirly heart on Valentine's Day. Her stomach dropped when she began reading, "*So sorry about your mom,*" "*Love and prayers,*" "*Your mom will be missed,*" and on and on. How did these people already know? Was it in the news? Carly hadn't told anyone but Lisa and Tyler.

Carly threw her phone down on the couch. She couldn't deal with any of it. The fact that people knew her mom had been murdered was devastating to her. In reality, she knew that people would eventually find out, but she wished she could hide it and never speak of it. Her dad found her pacing in the living room.

"What's going on?"

Carly threw up her hands. "Well, everyone knows, and it's all over social media!"

Her father puffed his cheeks and blew air out of his mouth. He looked stressed and older as if he had aged 20 years overnight.

"This is a nightmare, Daddy!" Carly said.

Carly's dad gathered her in his arms. "I'm so sorry, baby. I'm so sorry."

Carly sobbed once again, wondering how she had any tears left. "Why did they kill her, Daddy? Who would do such a thing?"

Her dad didn't speak, just continued to rub her back. Carly knew there were no words or reasons that would make this horrible situation make sense, but she couldn't help but ask *why*. Why did God let this happen? Lisa said she would pray that God would give her strength. Carly didn't feel any strength at that moment. She wanted to crawl in the bed and hide from the world. God had abandoned her in a time that she needed Him most. Carly wasn't able to deal with this farce, and no amount of praying would help her. If she was certain of anything, she was certain of that.

Later, at the police station, Detective Fuller took their statements separately. Carly told him all she knew, which wasn't much, but he said every little thing could be helpful. She asked him if he knew who could have killed her mother, and he informed her that, no, they didn't, but that they were doing everything they could to resolve the situation.

Her father seemed nervous as they left the station. Carly felt numb. Her grandmother had asked them to come by the house after they left the police station to talk about funeral arrangements. Carly dreaded it and didn't want to go. She told Tyler to meet her there when he left the farm.

Carly's grandparents were still sitting in the den, smoke swirling everywhere. "Come on in and eat something, dear," Gigi said. "My friends have been bringing in more food than we know what to do with, and it's covering every inch of the kitchen counter. The fridge is packed full. Poor Helena has been working herself silly in there. Can you just imagine all of Shelly's customers that are going to have to find a new beauty shop? Poor Myrtle will be devastated. I was just telling Frank that my hair needs a cut and color, and I have no idea what to do." Carly's grandmother wiped her eyes with a hanky. "Shelly always let me come in and get my hair done any time I wanted, and I never even needed an appointment. I just can't believe my Shelly Francis is dead!"

Pops was in his favorite recliner, a blanket covering his legs. Between the smoke and the warm house, Carly couldn't imagine needing a blanket. She was sweating with a sleeveless top and shorts on.

"Carly, I don't think your mother had any funeral arrangements planned, so we'll have to figure out everything," he said. "She couldn't have known that she would leave us so soon. Don't you worry about a thing. We'll use Weavers Funeral Home. They know us, and they'll take care of everything."

Carly nodded. "Okay, Pops."

"Do you want to pick out your mama's outfit for the casket, dear?" Gigi asked.

Carly looked in confusion at her grandmother. "An outfit?"

"Yes," she said. "You must pick out something in her favorite colors. She would have wanted that."

Carly tried to picture her mom lying in a casket, with an explosion of purple. She didn't know what her mom would have wanted, but Carly didn't want to even think about it. "Do we have to have an open casket? I just don't think—"

"Of course, we have to have an open casket," Gigi said. "That's what everyone expects. That way, everyone can say goodbye properly and have that visual effect. I went to a funeral not too long ago, and they had a closed casket with a picture on top of it. It just wasn't right."

"Gina, we don't have to have that," Pops said. "Can't you see that Carly is getting upset? Why do you have to go on and on about things that don't matter?"

"Who asked you, Frank?"

"Nobody. What do you think, Jared?"

Carly's dad looked extremely uncomfortable and shrugged his shoulders. "I don't think I have a say in this."

Gigi looked sweetly at Carly's father. "Jared, you know how I've always loved you, dear. I told Shelly repeatedly that leaving you was the worst mistake of her life, but of course, you know she never listened to me." After taking a deep puff and waving the smoke away, she said, "You will always be part of the family."

Carly felt claustrophobic. How was she going to survive this? She couldn't imagine anything worse than what was happening to her at that moment. "I just don't think Mom would want an open casket, Gigi," she said. "Besides, what if...what if she's been disfigured?"

"Don't you even worry about that," Gigi said. "Embalmers can do wonders. Why, you should have seen my friend Dee Dee after she died. She looked better than she did when she was alive. Didn't she, Frank?"

Carly's grandfather looked aghast. "She couldn't look any worse. I, myself, like funerals that are short and to the point. Those preachers need to save their soul-winning for church."

Carly listened to their banter back and forth, which made absolutely no sense to her, and tried to encourage a closed casket, but her grandmother was adamant and would have it her way in the end. Carly would sometimes give her opinions, but her grandmother said she had more experience and knew what was better. Carly finally gave up and let her do it her way. It gave her grandmother purpose and something to think about and plan.

Carly did think that if you were ever going to listen to a preacher about what could happen if you didn't know Jesus, a funeral would be the perfect time. Carly's mom didn't talk about Jesus much, even though she claimed to be saved. She only went to church sometimes, mostly to show off a new outfit. Gigi and Pops went most Sundays, but it was more for the social atmosphere. They went to the big Methodist church in town that boasted of the more prominent citizens of Bristol. The whole Sunday afternoon, conversations consisted of all the who's-who and the what's-what gossip.

Just when she thought she would go crazy with the whole bizarre business of funeral preparation, Tyler showed up and Carly was able to make her escape. She hugged her father goodbye and made plans to meet with him later. Tyler walked her to Matt's car, and they headed to Johnson City. Tyler held her hand in the back seat, but both brothers were unusually quiet on the drive home. Once Matt dropped them off at her place, Tyler escorted her inside.

Carly could tell something was bothering Tyler, something beyond the fact that her mother was murdered. "What's going on, Ty?" she asked.

Tyler sighed. "I know you're going through a lot right now, but there's something that I think you should hear from me."

Carly closed her eyes and braced herself for more bad news.

"First of all, my mom wanted me to tell you that she's so sorry about what happened to Shelly and that she loves you. She said to call her when you're ready to talk."

Josie still didn't know that Carly and Tyler were dating, but she did know they were best friends. Clearing his throat, Tyler continued, "I don't know how to tell you this. I'm sickened by it, and my brother is furious." Taking a deep breath, Tyler said, "My dad had an affair with your mom."

"What?" Carly said.

"Dad turned to Shelly when my mom was going through a rough time," Tyler said. "I'm not sure about much, but I do know that because of restraining orders placed against each other, my dad is a suspect in your mom's murder. Mom has forgiven him for the affair and says they all made mistakes. They both say that they had nothing to do with Shelly's death, but apparently, you're guilty until proven innocent."

"What do you think?" Carly asked.

Tyler took Carly's hands. "I believe them. There's no way that my dad or mom could do something like that."

Carly squeezed his hand back. "Then I believe them, too," she said. "I have something to confess to you, Ty. I knew something was wrong. I told you how crazy Mom was acting, and you saw it for yourself. She kept hinting around to me about John, but I thought she was just delusional. I never thought it went that far—at least, I hoped that it hadn't."

Tyler gathered Carly in his arms. "Good grief, girl, you smell like an ashtray!"

A giggle escaped Carly's mouth. "It's no wonder. You should have seen the mountains of cigarette butts. At least Pops went outside to smoke his cigar. There was no way I was eating any of that food. Can you take me to Pal's? I'm starving!"

Pal's was a fast food drive-thru, popular in east Tennessee and southwest Virginia.

Just being with Tyler was comforting. Carly didn't see how she could love him any more, but she did. Yes, she did love him. They hadn't said it to each other yet, but Carly knew that Tyler must love her too. Who else would put up with her?

# Chapter 31

## *Jared*

Jared felt like the lowest scum of the earth. Seeing Carly so traumatized and knowing he was the cause of it was more than he could bear. In one way, he didn't want to be around her, knowing what he had done, but he knew that if the truth came out, he might never have his daughter by his side again. This might be it for him.

The detective had asked him questions, and he could tell by the look in his eye that he was thinking some things didn't add up. First of all, Jared didn't have anyone to back up his alibi of being at home. When things got too personal, he had almost stopped and asked for a lawyer, but he thought that might make him look guilty. The detective wrapped it up but asked if they could download his cellphone data before he left. Jared didn't know what they would find on his phone, but he didn't think there would be anything incriminating. He had always deleted Shelly's texts messages and would have blocked her but didn't because of Carly. Sometimes, she would leave nasty voicemail messages, which he also deleted. He never answered when she called because all she wanted to do was yell at him.

After Carly had gone back to Johnson City, he tried to get on with his daily routine, but he figured his days were numbered. Somehow the truth would come out. It always did. He tried to function normally but ended up taking too many pills to help him forget. His stomach was on fire.

Fortified with the drugs and feeling like a fraud, Jared escorted his daughter to the funeral, which was packed wall to wall with people. Seeing Shelly lying there in one of her purple dresses made him want to vomit. Carly was visibly distressed, so they didn't linger long in the receiving line. Gina and Frank took charge and spoke with everyone who came. Gina confessed earlier that she was wearing a nicotine patch to help her make it through the day.

Jared noticed one of the detectives during the funeral service trying to appear detached, as if he wasn't watching every move everyone made. Jared didn't want to believe that he was being observed specifically, but he couldn't help it. He knew it wasn't just his imagination that one of the detectives was watching him like a hawk. He tried to ignore him and instead focused on being there for his daughter. Carly was heartbroken and overwhelmed. She shouldn't be going through something like this. What had he done?

Every person who spoke to him made him apprehensive. They were probably wondering why he was there because Shelly had hated the air he breathed and didn't mind telling anyone who would listen. He was relieved when Carly asked if he minded if she left with Tyler. Jared wanted to go home and take more pills to take the pain away, to make him forget that he killed his daughter's mother. He couldn't look in Carly's eyes anymore because the guilt was overpowering.

The next morning, Detective Fuller was banging on his door. Jared was surprised and didn't even put up any resistance when the detective placed him under arrest. It was over. He was finished. It was almost a relief.

# Chapter 32

## *Carly*

Carly looked at Tyler in astonishment. He had called her and said he was coming over, and that he had news about her mother's murder investigation. When he told Carly that her father had been arrested, she told him that it had to be a mistake. There was no way that her father could ever kill anyone, including his ex-wife.

Knowing Tyler would never hurt her for the world, Carly sat down, trying to explain to her boyfriend that it was impossible. "There has to be an explanation," she said. "Even if they arrested him, they're wrong. Sometimes they arrest the wrong people, right?"

"Matt said that they have some concrete evidence," Tyler said.

Carly stood up in anger. "My father did NOT kill my mother! That's all there is to it. They've made a huge mistake!"

Tyler was quiet while Carly paced in her small room. He had to see that it wasn't possible. She picked up her phone and called her dad, but it went straight to voicemail. "Daddy, please call me back as soon as you get this. I know you didn't do it. I love you, and I believe in you. Call me!"

"Do you want to talk to Matt?" Tyler asked.

"No! I don't want to talk to Matt! This is absolutely insane!" Carly took a deep breath. "Look, I'm not mad at you. You're just the messenger, but the detectives have it wrong. Whatever evidence they think they have is nothing. My father would *never* do that to me." Carly tried her best to explain the absurdity of the police thinking her father killed her mother. "You should have seen him, Tyler. He was so sad that Mom died, even after the way she had treated him for so long. They have no idea what they're talking about."

Knowing that there was nothing he could say or do, Tyler must have finally realized that she was right. "It's okay, Carly," he said. "I'll help you through this. I'm sure it will all be okay."

The next few days were absolute torture for Carly. Everyone believed her father was a murderer, and it was getting harder and harder to profess his innocence. She wanted to talk to her father but wasn't allowed to see him. Eventually, she was beginning to have her own doubts. Even her grandmother was saying Jared did it. Gigi said that they found the murder weapon in Jared's truck, which still had traces of blood.

"I always knew there was something not right about that man," Gigi said. She also said Jared's cell phone's tracking device placed him at the house on the night of the murder.

Carly couldn't be around her grandparents, or anyone else, except Tyler. They grew closer than ever. He was there when Carly finally accepted the fact that her father killed her mother.

"I've lost my mom, and I've lost my dad," she said. "He might as well be dead to me."

Tyler encouraged Carly to talk with his mother. He told her that she had been through a rough time, too. Josie found out that her dad, who had died recently of Alzheimer's, wasn't her real dad. She found her real father, and they were beginning to have a bond.

"I finally told her about us," Tyler said.

"You did? What did she say?"

"She asked me if I loved you."

Carly blinked. "And what did you say?" Carly wanted to hear it. She knew he loved her, had to love her, because her life would be nothing without it.

"I told her I was crazy about you, of course," Tyler said.

"But do you love me?" Carly asked.

"I have to say it?" Tyler rolled his eyes.

Carly slapped him on the arm. "Yes, you have to say it!"

"Okay, weirdo, I love you."

Carly smiled to herself, relishing the warm feeling of knowing how Tyler felt about her. Even though her life was unfathomable, hearing Tyler say those words meant she could go on. Her best friend in the universe loved her, and knowing he loved her would get her through the rest of her life. Hopefully, she would forget the miserable existence of the parents that raised her. She hated them both now. Lisa told her that she couldn't continue her life with that kind of hate, but Carly knew differently. As long as she had Tyler's love, everything would be fine.

"Well?" Tyler said.

Carly continued grinning. "Well, what?"

Looking frustrated, Tyler said, "Do you love *me*?"

Carly felt like she was getting ready to burst, and she tried to hold it in, but she couldn't. "Of course I love you, too, weirdo!"

# Chapter 33

## *Carly*

The next few months were very challenging and difficult. Once they had gone back to school, there were stares and whispers, which Carly tried to ignore. Why couldn't they just get over it? Carly was so frustrated. Her father had tried to contact her, but she just ignored him. His trial had been quick because of his confession. He was convicted of voluntary manslaughter and sentenced to 10 years in prison before being allowed parole. The state placed him in the River North Correctional Prison in Independence, Virginia. Carly didn't care where he was because she never wanted to see him again.

Carly's grandparents said they would pay for her tuition and all of her college expenses, which was a relief. Carly and Tyler would spend Sundays visiting them, as well as Josie and John. Carly finally met Josie's real father, David, and she thought he was pretty nice. John was distant when she first began spending time with them but now, he was like the old John. Josie was always there for her with open arms. Carly wasn't sure how they could be around her after what her parents had done, but she was thankful. Being with them brought some kind of normalcy to her existence.

Carly was still taking basic courses at school, but she had no idea what she wanted to do. The only thing she was good at was writing. She continued to keep a journal and took as many writing courses as possible. She wanted to focus on an English major but had no idea where she could take that degree. Tyler had settled on criminal justice, just like his brother, Matt.

Carly was self-conscious at school, being the girl whose father murdered her mother. People stared and whispered, but eventually, her notoriety began to diminish. Being a private person anyway, her attitude did not encourage anyone to approach her or dare ask personal questions.

Tyler felt like he was missing something, so he began talking more about church. He had always loved going with his family. Carly didn't discourage him from going anywhere, but she didn't encourage him either. Tyler had a good friend that kept asking him to attend the church on campus, so one day he decided to go and asked if Carly would go with him. She didn't really want to go. She was still mad at God and felt like He had abandoned her when she needed Him most. She went mostly for Tyler and pretended to be happy to be there but felt like such a fake.

Tyler loved it and soon began volunteering for different programs, encouraging Carly as well. Carly refused. She didn't know the Bible like Tyler did. She felt inferior and ignorant. Besides, how could someone with so much baggage help anyone else? She could only try to help herself, trudging day by day. Sometimes she felt bad for Tyler, like she was holding him back from bigger and better things. She didn't want to be a burden to him, but she couldn't let him go either. She could see that he loved everyone and that his faith was so strong. Tyler continued to love her, despite all the craziness and drama of her life.

Carly went to church with Tyler but kept everyone at arm's length. She didn't want to get close enough to tell anyone her business. Tyler didn't push her but encouraged her to tell her story because it would be a great testament. Poor Tyler thought she was managing her disfunction well, but he had no idea how bad it was. Sometimes she felt as if she wanted to kill herself, rather than continue on with her life. Only Tyler and his unconditional love held her back. What did she do to deserve him? That was the only good thing God ever did for her.

Tyler and Josie encouraged her to go and talk to her dad. Carly absolutely refused. She had nothing to say to him. When she thought of how he acted after her mother's death and now knowing what he had done, it was more than she could fathom. She could never forgive him. She could never forget the torment he had caused in her life. Her mom hadn't been any better. Carly had days when she still hated her. She would think of all the frustration over the years and blame Shelly for what happened. She could just imagine how her mom had driven her dad to murder. No, she didn't deserve to die, but she didn't help herself by pushing and pushing.

When Carly heard about how her mother had pursued John, she felt so much shame. What was her mom thinking? Did she really think John would leave Josie for her? Was she that crazy? Carly began to wonder if she would go crazy too. Would she end up in Marion like crazy Aunt Sally? Carly did her best to hide her hate, which instead of lessening was getting worse. Tyler deserved better than her.

After their second semester of school ended and summer began, Tyler mentioned to her that he was rethinking his career choice, which was a revelation. He told her he was beginning to realize that he wanted to be a pastor.

"What do you think?" Tyler asked.

"A pastor? Are you kidding me?" Carly said.

Tyler laughed as if something was funny. "Do you think you could be a pastor's wife?"

Carly panicked. They had never officially talked of marriage, although Carly couldn't imagine ever being with anyone else. "I would be the worst pastor's wife ever!" she said. "You know I hate people!"

Tyler's face fell. "I don't know why you say things like that," he said. "I know you don't hate people."

Carly loved the fact that Tyler thought the best of her. If he only knew how black her soul really was, he would never have anything to do with her. "Tyler, I thought you wanted to be a police officer," she said. "What happened to that?"

"I don't know. I just feel this calling. When God calls you to do something, He won't relent until you do it, but I can't do it without you." Tyler held Carly's hands. "I would think you'd rather I save souls that risk dying every day protecting citizens from criminals."

Carly pulled her hands back. She couldn't lose Tyler, but she couldn't stand in church pretending that everything was perfect, and God was real. In a panic, she turned her back on him. If she could do one good thing in her life, it would be to let Tyler go because he deserved someone so much better than her. He deserved that perfect girl who was lovely and sweet and everything that Carly wasn't.

"Tyler, I think we need a break," Carly said.

"Would you stop," Tyler said, sounding exasperated.

Carly shook off the hand that touched her shoulder. This would be the hardest thing she ever did in her life, but she had to do it. "I'm serious, Tyler. I've been thinking that we need to reach out and explore other options. I'm wondering if we need to see other people. Make sure that we're not missing something."

Tyler forcibly turned Carly toward him. "Carly, stop. I don't want anyone but you. This is stupid, and you know it."

Carly shrugged him away again and lied. "It's not stupid," she said. "We've known each other since we were babies. Sometimes you seem like more of a brother than a boyfriend."

Carly almost broke when she saw the look of devastation on Tyler's face. How could she hurt him like that? She could and she would save him from attaching himself to someone like her. He would be better off.

"Is it because I want to be a pastor?" Tyler asked.

"No! Of course not!" Carly said. "I've been thinking about this for a while." Her voice almost faltered, but she trudged on, "Actually, there's this guy who's been asking me out, and I really want to say yes."

There had been no guy, and there never would be. Carly would rather be by herself than with anyone but Tyler.

Carly finally began to see the anger in Tyler's eyes. Good. It was working. "Maybe it won't be forever, but we need to at least see," she said. "Don't be so mad about it. You'll be glad once you realize what I'm saying is for the best."

She tried to sound calm and casual, hiding the tremors that were in her voice. What would she do without Tyler?

Tyler picked up his ballcap and headed toward the door. "I'm leaving right now, but let me say, for the record, this is dumb," he said. "When you come back to your senses, call me."

Carly let him leave, not telling him that she wouldn't change her mind. It had to end now before he hated her. Sure, he was mad, but he still loved her. Once he found someone else, he would remember her fondly, as a friend. He would never know how hard it was for her to let him go. He would never know how much she loved him.

# Chapter 34

## *Carly*

After school let out, Carly began looking for an apartment close to campus. She found a one-bedroom that was reasonably priced and had a few amenities, such as a washer and dryer. It was time to move on from the Holloways. Once they had found out what had happened to her mother, they were never the same. They always looked at her funny, like they were worried they would be murdered next. Carly planned to work as many hours as possible at the café to pay for her new place. It gave her something to do to keep her mind off of Tyler. She was able to find used furniture and accessories at Goodwill and The Salvation Army.

Tyler would continue to call and text relentlessly. Sometimes, she would answer his texts in brief messages, but she never answered his calls. He finally told her he would give her the time she needed, but also informed her that he wasn't giving up.

Lisa gave her as many hours as she could at the coffee shop, trying to counsel her in the process. Carly tried to explain to her mentor and boss that it was impossible for her to continue to be in Tyler's life and bring him down to her level because he was one of the sweetest, kindest people on the planet. Nothing Lisa could say would change the truth.

When her junior year at ETSU began, Carly tried to avoid Tyler as much as she could. Again, she signed up for all the online classes available, hoping she wouldn't run into him. When she did see him on campus, her heart felt as if it was breaking.

One day, while walking to class, she saw Tyler walking with a girl. Her heart sank, and she ended up skipping her class and staying in her apartment for the rest of the day. He had every right to move on, especially when she was such a loser. He deserved someone good; she just wished that someone was her.

Carly wasn't the friendliest barista, but she tried her best to be as kind as she could. Most people just wanted their orders served promptly and efficiently. One autumn day, she finally went over the edge. One of their regulars, Mr. Harris, who Carly dubbed "Mr. Smarty Pants" came every weekday morning, at 7:50—no earlier and no later. He always wanted a large cup of the popular arabica coffee. He was so particular that it be fresh that he wanted to see the last coffee drips himself. They knew he was coming and tried to always time it so that it would be almost ready when he arrived.

That particular morning, Mr. Smarty Pants arrived about two minutes after the coffee had finished percolating. Carly was in a hurry and did it a minute or two before she usually did. She tried to tell him that it had just finished, but he obviously didn't believe her and demanded a new pot, lest they try to pawn old coffee off on him. He had to realize how they tried to accommodate him every day, but he must have been in a mood. Unfortunately for him, Carly was in a mood too.

"I'm telling you that this coffee is fresh," Carly said. "It just finished the cycle right as you walked in the door. There's no reason to make another pot."

Mr. Smarty Pants looked at Carly's badge. "There's every reason, but the only reason you need, *Carly*, is that I'm demanding a new pot."

Carly did her best to calm down before she went off on him. He had no idea with whom he was dealing. He could take his reasons and shove them up his skinny butt, which was covered in the most hideous, tight, acid-washed jeans that she had ever seen in her life. Carly was on her own, because Lisa was getting more half and half at the grocery store.

Carly pointed at the carafe and said in her most cynical tone, "Take it or leave it."

"Where is your manager?" he asked.

"I'm the manager at the moment, *sir*."

"Where is that other lady?"

"Obviously, she's not here right now. Do you want your coffee or not? It's getting older by the second." If he didn't hurry up, Carly was going to give him his coffee, and it wouldn't be in a cup.

"I don't want your coffee, now or ever," he said. "You have just lost a customer, and believe me, I will be giving the worst rating on Yelp that you could ever imagine, and I will specifically mention your name."

Not caring one bit, Carly shrugged her shoulders. "If that's what makes you happy, write your nasty review. I just wish I could write a nasty review about you!"

Carly knew she was going too far but couldn't help herself. He should just be glad that she wasn't jumping across the counter and stabbing him with one of the ink pens. Would he be scared knowing that her father was a murderer, and the victim was her mother? Would he be shaking in his tight little britches knowing what Carly might be capable of?

He must have seen the craziness in her eyes because he backed off and turned to walk out the door. Before he made it, Lisa came walking in with her milk.

"Hello, Mr. Harris," she said, "I hope you have a...great...day." Her sentence trailed off once she noticed the outraged look on his face. "Is everything okay?"

Mr. Harris stopped at the door. "I have never been so insulted in all my life. Needless to say, I will never darken your doors again." He stepped out but then stepped back in with the door still open to mouth his final words. "And this is not the last time you will be hearing from me."

With that final parting, he left in a huff.

Lisa came in with an anxious look on her face. "What in the world happened?" she asked.

Carly untied her apron and put it on the counter. Speaking slowly and distinctly, Carly said, "That man needs to be hog-tied and fed to the coyotes, and I'm just the person to do it."

Lisa shook her head.

"I've gone over the edge this time, so I'll turn in my notice so you don't have to fire me," Carly said.

Carly began walking to the breakroom while Lisa followed behind her. "I'm not firing you, but I do think you need to take a leave of absence to get it together. This has been coming for a while, and honestly, I've been expecting it any day." Lisa put her hand on Carly's shoulder. "Honey, you've got to talk to someone. You need some counseling."

Carly nodded. "Yes, I need something—whether it's counseling or something even more intense, like an extended stay in the looney bin."

"Have you talked to Tyler?" Lisa asked.

"No, and I'm not going to. I'm not going to ruin his life with all my drama. I'll just bring him down. He's better off without me."

"Carly."

"Look, I appreciate all of your help. I'll let you know what's going on. And I promise, I'll look for some kind of counseling. I don't know if it will help, but it sure can't hurt."

Carly stopped at the Pal's drive-thru on the way home, getting two large bags of cheddar rounds and a big peachy tea. As she ate, she thought that the cheesy potatoes and tea were all the therapy she needed. She could get a job there and hopefully get a discount on all the food she wanted. She could just imagine getting fatter and fatter, blowing up like Josie's pet pig, Wilmer. She'd end up having all of her fast food delivered to her room, never having to talk to another soul again. Food would be her friend until she died from extreme obesity.

Seriously, what was she going to do now? Her grandparents were helping her, but she couldn't expect them to give her more money. She had to have a job, but if she didn't get a grip, she was going to kill somebody. Like father, like daughter. It was in her blood.

Unexpectedly, Carly received a text from Josie.

**How are you? I haven't seen you lately. Are you and Tyler okay? Of course, he won't tell me anything.**

If Tyler hadn't told his mother of their breakup, she wasn't going to either.

**I'm fine, just been busy at work. Hopefully, I'll see you soon.**

Carly knew she didn't actually answer any questions, but she hated to lie any more than she had to.

Carly changed into jeans and a long-sleeved T-shirt for walking. She would go check on her grandparents and then, while in Bristol, walk on the trails at Steele Creek Park. She needed exercise and time to think about what she needed to do next.

Her grandmother answered the door with a grimace. "Come on in."

"What's wrong with your face, Gigi?" Carly asked. She had bandages on her forehead and one on the tip of her nose.

"Doc Shermer burnt some cancer off. I look like I got into a fight with a rooster and lost." Before Carly could sit down, her grandmother grabbed her pocketbook and continued, "Can you take me up to the Shell? I'm out of cigarettes."

Carly nodded, and they headed to her truck. "You need to quit, Gigi."

"I would if I could."

"Have you ever tried?"

"Ha! Only a million times."

Once they got to the station, Carly waited on her grandmother, who finally came out with two packs of cigarettes. "Why don't you get a carton?" Carly asked. "I'm sure it would be cheaper."

While buckling up, her grandmother said, "If I bought a carton, I'd smoke every one of 'em."

Carly figured that would be about right. "How's Pops?"

"He about burnt the house down the other day," Gigi said. "He left his cigar burning in his TV room. If Helena hadn't gone in there and saw the smoke, all his stuff would have gone up in flames."

The Shell station was only about five minutes from their house, so they were back in no time. Carly found her grandfather tinkering in the garage. He had on his University of Tennessee ballcap and T-shirt, and both looked a little worse for wear.

"Gigi told me about the cigar," Carly said. "Pops, you need to be careful."

He rolled his eyes dramatically and pointed at Carly's grandmother. "Pfft! She's the one that needs to be careful. I bet she didn't tell you how many times she's about burnt the bed up when she falls asleep with one of those ciggys in her mouth."

Carly's grandmother stopped and put her hands on her hips. "Why don't you quit running your mouth and get busy with those boxes of trash you need to take to the dump?" Gigi said.

Pops threw up his hands and looked at Carly. "You see what I put up with? She's going to put me in an early grave so she can collect on my life insurance."

Carly wasn't concerned about their bickering because that was the way they had always communicated. It was normal and somehow comforting in a weird sort of way. Carly knew they loved each other.

"By the way, dear, I Venmoed you some money," Gigi said.

Carly had taught her grandmother how to easily transfer cash instead of having to run to the bank and deposit it. "There wasn't much in the settlement of your mama's business, but it will help a little with your expenses," Gigi said.

Carly was surprised, knowing that her mom had left tons of debt. She hadn't expected much at all. Her grandfather had said not to worry about it; he had plenty of investments to cash in, and she also had money from the sale of her parents' house that her dad's lawyer set aside for her. With everything going on, she was glad that she, at least, didn't have to be concerned about money too.

Carly stayed for about an hour and left. She had been thinking about visiting her mother's grave and wondered if she had the courage to do it. Even though her mom was dead, she wanted to scream at her. She wanted to yell and get it all off of her chest. Maybe it would give her the closure she desperately needed.

Carly texted Josie and asked if she could tell her again where the gravesite was. Josie texted back, **It's at the very back, where the road ends. Do you want me to go with you?** Carly told her that she needed to do this by herself, but she appreciated the offer. Josie texted her to **just look for the purple flowers.**

Carly drove to the cemetery, dread settling in her stomach. She wasn't sure if it was the right thing to do, but she had to do it. She had to tell her mother how she had hurt her and how she had made her life miserable. Once she entered the gates, she drove to the back where Josie told her to park. She walked around and finally found the grave.

Carly knelt in front of the shiny stone that her grandmother designed and had made for Shelly. It was heart-shaped, with the words "*In Loving Memory*" and "*Never Forgotten*" engraved around her mother's picture, and a copper vase filled with various shades of purple silk flowers was in the middle of it. The photo was the one her mother used on all of her business cards. She used a professional photographer and had worn her signature purple. Her shoulder-length hair was styled, blonde, and teased to perfection.

Seeing the photo caused Carly's stomach to clinch. She couldn't believe Shelly had been gone for over a year. Sometimes it felt as if it had only been weeks or even days. The hurt was still so strong that it consumed her. Carly had just been a pawn in her parents' life. How could they destroy her like they did? Did she mean nothing to either one of them?

Carly looked at her mother's picture. "Why, Mom?"

She couldn't even voice anything else. There were so many questions she had for her mother, like why did she hate her father so much? Why did she obsess over someone else's husband? Why couldn't she be happy? Why was she never satisfied?

Carly closed her eyes and began grumbling, and then groaning. Eventually, she began shouting, "Why? Why? Why?" over and over again. She was sobbing until she couldn't cry anymore. She was done. She didn't think she felt much better, but she did feel relief. She looked around to see if anyone had noticed her little spectacle. There was a tree close by, and a squirrel was perched on one of the limbs staring at her.

"What are you looking at?" Carly stood up, brushing grass and dirt from her jeans. "I'm sure I'm not the first human you've ever seen shrieking at a tomb stone. Go mind your own business."

Carly began walking back to her truck, not caring where she stepped. She was still mad, still upset and still fed up. She would never live a normal life. She was sick of everything.

Not having anything else to do and no one to see, Carly decided to head to the park. After parking her truck, she put her key inside her shoe and began walking the trails that wound around a lake. She couldn't help but think of the times that she had spent there growing up, and also the times with just her and Tyler.

She passed a middle-aged couple on the trail holding hands. She nodded at them and thought how nice it would have been to grow older with Tyler. This past year, he had been keeping a scruffy beard, and she loved it. She wondered if he still had it or if he shaved it off. She hoped not. She loved him best when he wore an old, soft T-shirt and jeans. His legs were long, and he always looked so good from behind. He looked good from the front and the side, too. Carly tried to shake the mental images that her thoughts had conjured. She had to stop thinking about him so much. It only made her miss him more.

She saw a bench up ahead and decided to stop and rest. After sitting for a few moments, she eventually pulled her legs up and wrapped her arms around them. Carly again tried not to think of Tyler, but she failed miserably. He was all she ever thought about. Not being able to talk and text every day was killing her. He had the same quirky sense of humor, and they would banter about the most absurd things like "the worst jobs ever." They would go back and forth for days, touting jobs like pet food taster, or portable toilet cleaner, or her favorite, animal masturbator. Tyler didn't believe it until he looked it up.

"I don't even want to know how you know that," he had said.

"I know things," she had replied.

Carly heard it somewhere, and when you hear something like that, you didn't forget it.

Tyler knew of every eccentric customer at the café, including one weird lady who said, "Steam Queen," every time you asked for her name to write on the cup. He also loved Carly's weirdness, like when she told him she shaved her big toe. He just assumed that her toes were smooth and not hairy like a man's. Her toes weren't as bad as his, but she did have a few hairs on the big one. She also admitted to him that her arm pits weren't the only place where she put deodorant but wouldn't elaborate any further, even though he begged her.

She also remembered how Tyler rubbed her feet when they ached and the way he kissed her, as if she were the most precious person in the world. He should have been with her when she went to the cemetery. He would have held her, comforted her, and made everything better, and then he would have bought her a blizzard from Dairy Queen knowing how much she loved them.

Carly closed her eyes. She had to stop. Going to the park was supposed to take her mind off all of the things that reeked in her life, including losing Tyler, her job, and parents—not make it worse. She could feel her throat tightening up. Oh, no.

Carly begged God, *If you're out there, God, please don't let me start crying right here. There are people on this trail, and they don't want to see a pitiful excuse for a human being crying her eyes out. Please, God! Please!*

As usual, she was on her own. God wasn't there, and He never would be. Hiding her face, Carly tried to look casual instead of the sniveling idiot she was. She didn't even have a hanky to wipe the snot pouring out of her nose. Carly began shaking in frustration. Maybe she should just end it. She just couldn't think of anything to live for.

# Chapter 35

## Carly

Carly felt someone sit down beside her. Maybe if she ignored them, they would go away. She tried to discreetly wipe her nose and face with her T-shirt.

"Here's a tissue. It's clean."

Carly, while keeping her head down, held her hand out, and a lady (judging by the sound of her voice) put a tissue in it. She slowly slid her legs down, while dabbing her nose and eyes.

"Thanks," Carly said.

"You're welcome. Come here a lot?"

Great, a talker—just what she needed. "Sometimes," Carly said. "I actually live in Johnson City."

*Way to go, Carly, just tell everyone where you live. When they find your dead body, you'll have nobody to blame but yourself.*

"This is my first time. It's beautiful here, isn't it?"

Carly, feeling frustrated, took a deep breath and wondered about what kind of person was determined to talk to her when she clearly didn't want to be bothered. Carly, doing a quick side view, wasn't good with age, but she decided this bothersome person was older than her mother and younger than her grandmother.

"Yes, it is," Carly said.

"I heard it's supposed to turn colder next week, so it's a good thing we're here today, don't you think?"

Carly didn't have time to talk to a weird chatty stranger, and she was about to tell her that when she looked into her eyes. Something stopped Carly in her tracks. The woman had the most unusual shade of blue eyes she had ever seen. They were almost too bright to look at. Carly was mesmerized, and the speech she was ready to spew forth just vanished.

"Yeah. I guess it is."

"It's a good day to thank God," the woman said.

Carly watched her close her eyes and look as serene as anyone had ever looked in their life. She even had a little smile that spoke of such a love that Carly almost began crying anew. How could anyone look that happy in a world that was so full of evil?

Carly began crying softly, unable to stop herself. The lady gently took her hand and brought it to her heart.

"Let it out, honey, but you can't cry forever," the woman said.

Confused and astonished, Carly felt as if this woman, who she had just met, knew everything about her.

"Life has thrown you some difficult challenges, but you're strong. You have people who love you, but most of all, you have the love of God, who will never turn his back on you. He's *always* there for you."

Carly felt love radiating from her hand. *What was going on?*

Carly was thinking that God couldn't love her, and before she could voice it aloud, this lady surprised her and said, "God does love you, more than you can ever fathom, but you have to accept His love. You are so special to Him, and He wants you to love yourself too. You can't love others until you love and accept yourself."

"But I'm—"

"Why haven't you turned to Him? God knows you, Carly. He knows everything about you. He knows how many hairs are on your head and what you think. There's nothing that He doesn't know."

"But how can He love me?" Carly genuinely wanted to know.

"Because He *is* love, holy and indescribable, and because you are His child. He created you."

For the first time in her life, Carly felt that love. She felt all the warmth pouring through her body. She closed her eyes as the lady beside her had done, smiling for the first time in a long time. God loved her. God really loved her, and she felt it through and through for the first time in her life. Turning to the special lady beside her, she wanted to thank her, but she was gone. Carly looked around, but she was nowhere in sight.

A jogger came running by, and Carly jumped up and stopped him. "Did you just see a lady right here?" she asked.

The jogger kept running in place. "No, just you."

Carly looked dumbfounded. What just happened? How could someone just disappear like that? It wasn't like the lady was young or anything.

"Are you okay?" the jogger asked.

"Yeah. Sorry. Thanks, I'm just a little confused right now."

She watched the man continue jogging until he went around the bend. Carly didn't know what just happened, but she did know that she felt so much better. She began walking back toward her car when it hit her. How did that lady know Carly's name?

# Chapter 36

## Carly

Feeling better than she had felt for a long time, Carly looked around, and instead of being dreary and drab, the world looked beautiful and bright. The trees were in their peak autumn colors, which were amazing and incredible. The lake was glistening, filled with happy, honking geese. The birdsong was like music, and the sky was the most exquisite blue that she could have ever imagined; puffy clouds sprinkled here and there.

Carly actually wanted to skip. Skip! She hadn't skipped since she was a little girl. Carly, Tyler, and Matt used to have skipping races at the farm. They would skip up the hills in the pasture and then run back down, trying their best to avoid all the cow patties. She would lose every time because she couldn't stop laughing at the boys, trying their best but looking awkward and ridiculous.

By the time Carly reached her car, she felt as if she was floating in happiness. Once she sat down and buckled her seat belt, she thanked God. She thanked him especially for his love and speaking to her in such a wondrous way when she needed it so badly. She knew God was real. She felt it in every fiber of her being. He was real, and He loved her. Her! Carly!

Now that Carly was coming down from her high, she asked herself, "Now what?"

She had to giggle. How did God put up with the human race? Really. He had to think that they were all a bunch of imbeciles. Carly began to think of Tyler and wanted to be with him, had to be with him. What was she thinking when she turned him away? Was it too late for them? Had he already moved on? The only way she would find out was to reach out, so Carly began texting.

**Hey.**

In seconds, Tyler was responding. *Hey.*

Carly smiled. She loved him so much and wanted to shout it out but also wanted to do it the right way. **Are you busy later? Can I see you?**

Carly noticed the responding three dots, and then nothing. Instead of panicking, Carly began praying, *Please, God, don't let it be too late for us.*

Instead of crying, Carly felt at peace. No matter what, God would be there for her. Tyler would always be her friend, even if it were too late for anything else.

Carly jumped when her phone vibrated on her leg. She looked and smiled.

**When and where?**

**My place. 7:00.** That would give Carly time to get home and shower and to also think about what she wanted to say and do.

**See you then. Weirdo.**

Carly responded with a smiley face.

Later, when the knock finally sounded on her door, Carly was nervous. Taking a deep breath, she opened the door, and Tyler stood there, neither smiling nor frowning, but looking serious.

"Come in." Carly opened the door wider and pointed to the couch. "Do you want anything to drink?"

Tyler shook his head. "No."

Carly took a deep breath. She could tell that there would be no chit-chat. Tyler wanted to know what was going on, and he didn't want to wait. He had that look in his eyes that she knew so well. One of the few faults he had was his impatience.

"I went to see Mom's grave," Carly began.

"Did it help?" Tyler asked.

"Not really. I yelled and screamed, and some squirrel watched me, waving his tail. I told him to mind his own business."

Tyler's mouth twitched, but he refused to smile. "Why am I here, Carly."

Carly could count the number of times on one hand that she had cried in front of Tyler. Looks like she was going to have to add a hand, because she could feel it bubbling up inside her.

"After I left the cemetery, I went to Steele Creek. This lady, I think she must have been an angel or something, because...because she told me things."

Tyler looked concerned. "What things?"

"First of all, she knew my name, and I never told her what it was." Even if Tyler wouldn't sit down, Carly knew she had to. Her legs felt as if they were about to give out. She sat down and pulled one of the pillows against her stomach and held it. "She told me that God knew me, knew everything about me, and He loves me, Tyler. He loves me because He is love. She said that I had to love myself, too, or I couldn't love anyone else." Carly smiled through her tears. "I felt that love, Tyler, and it was so strong. It was amazing. But then she disappeared. She was gone in an instant."

Tyler sat beside Carly but didn't touch her. Carly wanted him to touch her. She wanted it so much. If he didn't touch her soon, she would die.

"Tyler, I'm so sorry." Carly hung her head, crying her eyes out.

She didn't know what else to say.

Finally, Tyler pulled Carly into his arms, kissing the top of her head, the sides of her face, her nose, and then her lips. They kissed and kissed, making up for lost time. His kisses were sweet and demanding, gentle and strong. Eventually, they had to come up for air.

"I've missed you so much," Tyler said.

"I've missed you, too."

"I didn't think you would ever come back."

"I didn't think I ever could."

"My life has been miserable without you."

"Your life? My life has been more depressing than Toy Story 3!"

Tyler laughed. "That bad?"

"But better now. So much better. Can you ever forgive me?" Carly took his shirt and wiped her nose.

"Hey! This is a clean shirt," Tyler said.

"Well, get used to it, buddy. I've become a bleating goat." Carly looked at him seriously. "Can you? Can you forgive me, Ty?"

"As long as you never leave me again," Tyler said. "I'm serious, Carly. I can't take it. My life is nothing without you in it. I've been thinking about that pastor thing. If you're not comfortable with it, it's off the table."

Carly almost melted. He would actually give that up for her. But she would never let that happen. "No, I will do my best to be a good pastor's wife, like being nice to the old wrinklies and stuff." Carly stopped. "Wait a minute. You never even *asked* me to marry you."

Tyler grinned and proceeded to get down on his knee. He took her hand and pretended to put a ring on her finger.

Carly rolled her eyes. "That's the wrong hand, doofus." She held out her left hand instead.

"Anyway, Carly Francis, will you make me the happiest man on the planet and agree to be my wife?" Tyler asked.

Carly squinted and pursed her mouth, as if she was thinking about it. "I guess. But let me warn you that I'm not always in a good mood. I'm sometimes hateful, and I'm a lot messy."

"Unfortunately, I know all of that, and also unfortunately, I still want to marry you."

They both smiled at each other. At that moment, Carly felt as if she was the happiest human being on the planet. God and Tyler, knowing her, loved her anyway, flaws and all. What a wonderful feeling to know that. That's all she needed.

"So, I was thinking," Tyler said.

"What were you thinking?" Carly asked. She was thinking she was hungry, and a big, greasy cheeseburger would be a great ending to the day.

"Why don't you go and see your dad? I'd be glad to go with you."

# Chapter 37

## *Carly*

Carly didn't think that anything could cause her to not be happy on that happiest day on the earth, but Tyler's words, "Why don't you go and see your dad?" were the *anything*.

Carly's smile turned to a frown. "Why would you say that?"

Tyler didn't say anything for a few seconds, but she could tell that he wasn't going to let it go.

"Seriously, why would you say that?" Carly asked. "I can't talk to him. It's impossible."

"Why?" Tyler said.

"Because he killed my mother!"

"Don't you need answers? Don't you want to ask him why?"

In frustration, Carly yelled, "There's no reason that would be good enough, Tyler! I, of all people, know what kind of person my mother was, but she didn't deserve to be murdered."

"Of course she didn't, but he's still your father, and I know how much you loved him. I also know how you are, and that you won't be able to get on with your life without at least speaking to him."

Carly tried to be calm when all she wanted to do was scream. How could Tyler expect her to speak with him? As far as she was concerned, she had no father. She could never forget what he did or forgive him.

"Look, I'll be okay, eventually," Carly said. "I just need more time. As long as I have you, Tyler, I'll be okay."

Tyler pulled Carly into his arms. "You'll always have me."

Carly squeezed back. "Promise?"

"I wasn't the one that broke up with you, remember?"

Tyler tried to look at Carly, but she hung her head, muffling into his chest, "I didn't want to break up. I did it for you."

"Next time, don't do me any favors, okay?"

"Okay."

In the next few weeks, Carly was able to put one foot in front of the other because of Tyler, but mostly because she still felt God's love. She felt more at peace, but sometimes, in an angry moment, she would lose it. It was usually something stupid like getting in the wrong line. One day, she was in a hurry and decided to run through the car wash, and she quickly realized that many people had the same idea that day. Apparently, one of the cars ahead of her didn't know how to use the kiosk. She was stuck, not being able to go around him, and sat watching the other line speed swiftly along. As each car went ahead of her, she fumed. She tried to take deep breaths to calm down, but her anger was palpable. If the line hadn't begun moving when it did, Carly wasn't sure what she would have done, but it scared her.

Tyler didn't say anything else about Carly going to see her father in prison, but she knew that he was still thinking about it. She put on a good front, hoping he would see that she was dealing with her life trauma in an effective way, hiding the worst moments. Sometimes it was easy, but sometimes it was incredibly hard. If people knew what she was thinking, they would definitely run the other way. She prayed to God, but she knew she needed more help. She was having trouble sleeping and having the occasional nightmare. Usually, her dreams consisted of yelling and fighting with her mother. She would wake up with an unbelievable amount of frustration, feeling suffocated and overwhelmed.

Carly talked to her school counselor, who knew a little bit about her situation. She referred her to a couple of different therapists and encouraged her to make an appointment. On one particularly difficult day before Thanksgiving, Carly found the information and called to set up an appointment. She had to talk to someone, and she didn't feel that her boyfriend could manage the intensity of her feelings. After canceling the appointment a couple of times, Carly finally showed up, but with a great deal of trepidation.

The office was close to campus and on the second floor of an older building. Not seeing anyone in the waiting room, Carly sat down in one of the chairs. There were various magazines and pamphlets lying around haphazardly on the coffee table. Instead of picking one up, Carly pulled out her phone and began scrolling. A lady, who looked to be in her 30s, opened a door and walked softly towards her, visibly pregnant.

In a soft voice, she introduced herself, holding out her hand. "Carly? I'm Andrea. So nice to meet you."

Carly nodded nervously. "Nice to meet you, too."

Andrea motioned for Carly to follow her into another room. As Carly walked in, she noticed a couch right away and pictured herself lying there, looking at the ceiling, the therapist sitting beside her, saying, "And how does that make you feel?"

"Have a seat."

Not wanting to feel vulnerable, Carly chose one of the available chairs instead of the couch. She was determined not to cry and moan. She would get a few things off of her chest, and if that didn't work, on to the next thing, like changing her diet or trying yoga. She could get a service dog, like a mean little chihuahua that would growl at anyone who looked at her sideways.

"I'm so glad you made it in today," Andrea said. "I noticed from your intake forms that you've had a significant traumatic experience. I have another form that will help me better understand how that experience has affected you. Would you be willing to fill that out today? It only takes about five minutes."

Carly nodded. "Sure."

Andrea walked to a table and pulled out a clipboard with a form on it. After handing her the form and a pen, she said, "I'm going to let you fill this out, and I'll be back shortly."

After she left, Carly looked at the form, which had a list of responses that one might have to life experiences. They were rated 1-5, beginning with "not at all" to "extremely." The car wash incident would have definitely been an "extreme" angry outburst response. Carly read each one and answered with the best of her ability, with most responses being "a little bit" or "moderately." Evidently, having trouble sleeping and physical reactions such as heart pounding and trouble breathing because of her trauma experience was a thing, and she checked "extreme" in both cases.

Andrea reentered the room. "Do you need more time?"

Carly shook her head. "No."

After handing the form back to Andrea, Carly sat nervously while the therapist studied the form. "What I see here is quite normal for what you've gone through," Andrea said. "There are a lot of coping mechanisms we can suggest that have been very successful with many of our patients."

Carly let out a breath that she had been holding.

Andrea smiled reassuringly. "I think with a minimal number of sessions, you'll be fine, Carly. Just keep an open mind, and I'll help you get through it."

Carly felt that she was stepping in the right direction. Andrea helped her see how her experience had affected her well-being—mentally, emotionally, physically, and spiritually. Fortunately, she could heal and recover from the trauma in her life, and eventually she'd be able to understand, cope, and process her emotions. Unfortunately, it wouldn't happen overnight. Carly was okay with that, as long as there was a light at the end of the tunnel.

After that first session, Carly felt as if a huge burden had been lifted from her shoulders. She drove to the café to talk to Lisa and to let her know she was okay. The café was busy, which wasn't surprising, being a few weeks before Christmas. As Carly walked in, the holiday coffee aromas made her instantly crave something hot and sweet.

Lisa smiled when she saw Carly saunter in. "Well, it's about time!" After smiling, Lisa gave her a perturbed look. "You had me worried to death."

Carly, looking contrite, said, "I know. I'm so sorry. I wanted to see you and let you know that I'm okay."

Lisa came from behind the counter and put her arm around Carly. "Let's go in the back and talk." Once she got the front covered, they walked to Lisa's office.

"Now, tell me what's going on," she said.

Carly sat in one of the comfortable chairs and crossed her legs. "Again, I'm sorry about Mr. Harris."

"Pfft! Good riddance. As you can tell from out front, it didn't hurt the business any. We've been crazy busy with the holidays."

Carly smiled. "That day I left was a remarkably interesting day. I went to the cemetery, and then I went to the park and talked to an angel."

"A what?" Lisa said.

Carly laughed at the dumfounded expression on Lisa's face. "Yeah. It was definitely an experience I'll never forget." Carly raised her eyebrows. "I don't know if she was a real angel, but one minute she was there, knew my name, told me how much God loved me, and then poof! She was gone."

Lisa looked skeptical.

"I know," Carly said. "It sounds...bizarre, but there it is. After talking with her, I felt like I was walking on a cloud. I called Tyler. We got back together, and overall, it's been much better, but I knew I needed more help, so I finally met with a therapist. Actually, I just left from my first appointment. It was very enlightening and encouraging, and I plan to go back as long as I need to."

Lisa put her hand on her heart. "Oh, honey, that makes me so happy! I was so worried about you."

"I was worried about myself."

"You know you will always have a job here, whenever you're ready to come back."

Carly told Lisa she was ready and made plans to come in as soon as her first semester exams were over. Tyler was working that night, so Carly went home and cleaned her apartment. Then, she studied, waiting for him to swing by after his shift ended at nine. He was going to bring pizza and find out how her appointment went.

While she was waiting, Carly couldn't stop thinking about her father, which brought an aching dread to the pit of her stomach. Would talking to him be painful? Would anything he said really matter in the end? For the first time since she found out that her dad killed her mother, Carly felt like she needed and wanted to know why he did what he did. It was finally time.

# Chapter 38

## *Carly*

The closer they got to Independence, Virginia, where her father was incarcerated, the more nervous Carly got. Many times during the drive, Carly wanted to tell Tyler to turn around, that it was a big mistake, but she held her tongue. She hadn't gone this far with her recovery just to give up. Andrea, her therapist, had encouraged Carly to talk to her father but to leave at any point that she felt threatened or too uncomfortable.

Carly barely saw the bleak landscapes and sun peeking through the barren trees along the roadside. She wore her warmest coat because of the cold temperatures, which were accompanied by a strong north wind. Tyler had asked her several times if she was okay. Finally, she snapped.

"I'm fine! Stop asking me that," Carly said.

After a few moments of silence, Carly apologized, "I'm sorry. Obviously, I'm not fine." More silence. "I shouldn't have had those donuts, because I feel like I'm going to throw up."

"These roads are kind of curvy."

"Tyler?"

"Yeah?"

"Did you forgive your dad?"

Tyler had seemed good around his father, but Carly knew how he loved his mother and how close they were. Josie had forgiven John, but Carly wasn't sure Tyler and Matt had.

"I mean, yeah, I guess," Tyler said. "I try not to think about it because as long as Mom's happy, it's not my business, right?"

"Are you mad at him?" Carly had been mad. If Tyler cheated on her, she didn't think she could forgive him, and he would definitely regret it.

Tyler nodded. "Yes. I was, and if I'm honest, I guess I still am."

"Your mom is a better person than me, Tyler. I don't think I could ever get over that. I saw you one day on campus walking with another girl. I know we weren't together, and I would have no right to be mad if you were with someone else, because I broke up with you. I'd still be mad, though."

Tyler took Carly's hand. "Look, you don't have to worry about that. I don't even know who you're talking about. Besides, I knew you'd come around eventually, and if I made the mistake of going out with someone else, you'd beat us both up."

Carly giggled. "That's what I love about you, Ty."

"What? That I'm a pushover?" Tyler said.

Carly squeezed Tyler's hand and brought it to her lips. "No," she said. "It's that you love me even though I can be a little deranged sometimes."

Carly wanted to ask Tyler to pray with her but was embarrassed. She closed her eyes and prayed silently, asking God to give her strength and wisdom.

Before she exited the car, Tyler pulled her back for a hug. "You'll be fine. God will be with you the whole time; just lean on Him."

Carly nodded and smiled. She thought about a poem she read once at Tyler's grandmother's house. It was called, "The Footprints of God." She couldn't remember the whole poem, but it was about someone walking on the beach and noticing that while talking to God there was only one set up footprints in the sand during the worst times of their life. They asked why God left them during the tough times, and God answered that He didn't leave them but carried them instead.

As Carly headed toward the prison, she whispered, "Commence to carrying me, God. I need you now more than ever."

Carly never thought she'd ever enter a prison, much less visit her father in one. She had registered beforehand, so he knew she was coming. She left everything in the car except for her identification, telling Tyler to wait for her there.

Taking a deep breath, Carly entered the facility. Besides being nervous, she was cold, because she did not want to wear her heavy coat in the facility. Carly was told to place her identification into a locker. She didn't wear a belt or any jewelry because she knew in advance that she would go through a metal detector. Once she was scanned, Carly was physically searched. She had to open her mouth and lift her shirt and bra. She felt invaded and embarrassed, but she also knew it was a necessity.

By the time she got to see her father, she was shaking. He looked awful, and that broke her heart. The anger and hatred she had felt for so long seemed to vanish with one look. This was her daddy, who she had loved and still loved. Yes, she hated what he did, but she loved him. She began crying uncontrollably.

"Oh, baby, I'm so sorry," Jared said.

Carly couldn't help it. She cried and cried, but it was something she needed to do because she had held it in for so long. In a way, she was glad that that there was a no-touch policy but, in another way, she wanted to be held by her father. She wanted him to hold her like he used to when she was a little girl, and he would make everything feel better.

She grabbed the tissues that she placed in her jeans pocket, wiping her eyes and nose. "You look awful," Carly said.

"It's not a very uplifting place, but it's where I deserve to be," her father replied.

"Are you sorry, Daddy?" Carly asked. "Do you wish you hadn't done it?"

Jared closed his eyes and nodded his head. He then looked into Carly's eyes. "I'm sorry every day."

"But why did you kill her?"

"Carly, to be honest, I don't know," he said. "I just...did it. I was mad. I was angry. I was high."

"Why were you angry?" she asked.

Jared sighed. "She had been threatening to turn me into the IRS and told me that night that she already had. She also threatened to tell everybody terrible things about me. I threatened to tell Josie about her and John, but she laughed and said they already knew. When she laughed, I just lost it."

Carly's mom had always alluded to something bad in her father's life. She wasn't sure she wanted to know, but she asked anyway. "What terrible things? Drugs?"

Looking pained, her father pleaded with his eyes. He covered his mouth and looked away. "That, but other things too," he said.

"What, Daddy? What was so bad?" Carly asked.

"Carly, there are things that you don't want to know. It has nothing to do with you, but it's something I've lived with since I was a young boy."

"Is it why you sometimes look so sad?"

Jared nodded.

"And Mom threatened to tell everyone this bad thing? You killed her for it?"

"Yes," Jared said. "I guess I did. Your mom was disappointed in me, and I had failed her in our marriage. She couldn't get over it and always hated me for it."

Carly wanted to demand that her father tell her what it was, but she decided to back off. Maybe he was right, and she didn't want or need to know.

"One day I'll tell you, but not right now, okay? I was wrong, whatever reason I had for doing it. I'm sorry for everything that I've put you through. I'm sorry for taking your mom's life. She didn't deserve it, and I deserve to pay for what I did."

Carly knew he was right, but she couldn't help but feel sorry for him.

"I was surprised that you even wanted to see me here," Jared said "This is no place for you, and I hate that you came here. But I'm also glad because I've missed you. No matter what has happened, I love you more than anything in this world, and I always will."

Carly took a deep breath. "Tyler asked me to marry him."

Jared smiled. "I'm glad. I've always liked him. I hope you will be happy. That's all I ever wanted for you, Carly."

"Did you ever love Mom?" Carly wasn't sure what prompted her to ask that question, because it just popped out of her mouth. It would be nice to know that there was love between her parents at one time in their life. Was she conceived through love, indifference, hate?

"I was crazy about your mom," Jared said. "I loved her, and I think she loved me, but we were doomed by our past. Neither one of us could forget events in our lives that shaped us and made us who we were. I wish we could have done better, tried harder. We both failed you, especially me."

As Carly left the prison, she felt as if a huge burden had been lifted from her shoulders. Seeing her father in prison had been the right thing for her to do. It might have been different if he felt as if he didn't deserve to be punished for killing her mom.

Andrea had encouraged Carly to use her writing as a tool for expressing her emotions. At times, the anger would spew forth from her in scary spurts of reaction to all that she had endured. Other times, sorrow would overwhelm her. Lately, though, she had been more accepting of actions and consequences, and the feeling of redemption felt liberating and freeing.

Knowing that God had redeemed her was the catalyst that turned her whole life around. God had saved her. When she thought that she was all alone and He wasn't there, God was definitely carrying her through those challenging times. She couldn't control the actions of her parents, but she could control her own reaction toward them.

Carly learned through her walk with God that she wasn't like everyone else, but that's what made this entire world work. Everyone had their faults, but everyone also had their talents and gifts. God would help her with her impatience and use her past experiences to reach out to others. She was excited about what He had in store for her.

Carly knew she deserved nothing, but because Jesus gave his life, she was rescued and saved.

# Chapter 39

## *Jared*

Jared watched his daughter leave, trying his best to hold in his feelings. When he received the notification that she would be visiting him, he had mixed emotions. He wanted to write and tell her not to come but, in the end, he just couldn't do it. He needed to see her. He missed her, and he wanted to apologize for everything.

He was prepared for her judgement, and he knew he deserved whatever anger and resentment she felt for him. Instead, his daughter showed him compassion and love. He couldn't believe it. He was so overwhelmed that if he didn't make it back to his cell soon, everyone would see him break down and cry like a baby.

For the first time in a very long time, Jared had hope. He had hope for the future. What more could he ask for?

# Chapter 40

John watched Josie's face as Tyler and Carly announced that they were getting married. Tears of joy streamed down her face at the wonderful news. John closed his eyes, thankful once again that Josie had forgiven him. He just couldn't fathom a life without her and his boys.

Josie jumped up and down, hugging both Tyler and Carly alternately, squealing out loud. John hugged Carly and then shook his son's hand.

"We're so proud of you, son."

Tyler grinned and placed his arm around Carly's shoulders. "Thanks, Dad."

"Cherish her always."

It was John's turn to place his arm around Josie's shoulders. He looked at her as he spoke to Tyler and Carly. "Always take care of her, because you'll find that your life would be nothing without her."

# Epilogue

Has the LORD redeemed you? Then speak out! Tell the others he has redeemed you from your enemies.

— PSALM 107:2

Carly and Tyler got married after graduating from ETSU. Tyler began attending a seminary school, while Carly found a job as a Medical Transcriptionist. Carly needed a job that allowed her to work from home, and also to work on her new book. She had decided to write about her own life so that someone else might receive help because of everything she had gone through since she was a little girl.

Tyler had encouraged her to write and tell her story to the churches that he had been asked to be a guest pastor at. They worked as a team, which was more rewarding than anything Carly could have imagined. Because of her increased faith, she was more confident and poised in her demeanor. Knowing that she could help someone and encourage them was the gift that kept on giving. The more she could help, the more it helped her.

That day that Tyler had told her he wanted to be a pastor scared her to death. Carly thought that being a pastor's wife meant purity, which was not something that she envisioned of herself. Now she knew that, because of what she had gone through, her contributions were so much greater than she could have ever imagined.

When the time came for Tyler to be pastor of his own church, she knew she would be ready. She also knew that she would never be perfect, but that was okay. Her biggest obstacle would be overcoming her shyness at meeting new people.

Tyler would be the perfect pastor. He was funny, sincere, and his heart was so pure. Knowing that he loved her like he did made Carly always want to be a better person. He valued her opinions and critiques, even when he didn't abide by them, like wrapping his sermons up at twelve o'clock on the dot.

"I can't just stop because someone is hungry," he would say to her suggestion.

"I'm just telling you that, after a certain time, they're more worried about filling up their stomachs than listening to your fourth 'come on down,'" Carly said.

"Is that the way you feel?" Tyler asked.

"If I'm honest, yes. The more my stomach growls, the more I'm tuning you out." Carly was always honest with Tyler, and she wouldn't stop now just because he was a pastor.

Tyler rolled his eyes. "Being hungry is not the worst thing in the world."

Carly grinned. "I'm not the only one that's hungry."

"When I begin hearing a bunch of stomachs carrying on and people looking at their watches, then I'll know it's time."

"You won't be able to hear the tiny little stomach inside my big belly growling," Carly said.

Tyler shook his head and began walking off, then abruptly stopped. As he turned around, his face was comical, causing Carly to laugh. She nodded enthusiastically.

"Yep!" Carly said. "We're going to have a baby." She pulled Tyler close, whispering in his ear, "You'll be the best daddy ever."

# Acknowledgments

Thank you, Janie, Draco, Allison, and Tara at Jan-Carol Publishing! Your encouragement and support mean everything to me.

Thank you, Kenny Bruce, my husband and editor, for keeping me straight in between all of your farm chores.

Thank you to our boys, Adam and Sam; their wives, Tif and Catherine; and our grandchildren, Theodore, Evie, Lily, and Rosie. My children and grandchildren always inspire me in such creative and fun ways.

Thank you to my precious mother and stepfather, Wanda and Tom Sheppard. Your love and support keep me going, and I couldn't do it without you. I love you *way as the sky!*

Thank you to my daddy in heaven and my stepmother, Evelyn. We cling together in our memories of the man we both adore.

Thank you to my sister-in-law, Deborah Corn, for your extremely helpful feedback. You're always honest and supportive, and I love you for it.

Thank you, Cassy Corn, my niece, for your thought-provoking suggestion that the story wasn't over.

Thank you to everyone who took a chance on me by buying my books. I love each and every one of you and appreciate it more than I can ever convey in mere words. If you have the time and a few words to share, I would love to hear your thoughts and reviews through your preferred online book vendor or Goodreads.

Thank you to my church family at Victory Baptist Church in Bristol, Virginia. Your amazing support and love have been phenomenal.

And thank you most of all to my Father, in Heaven, who gives me the words and vision that I aspire to. I give Him all the praise and Glory.

# About the Author

Karen Bruce and her husband, Kenny, spend their days on their small farm in Mendota, Virginia. They enjoy time with their two children and four grandchildren. Her published works include *Josie: A Story of Forgiveness* and *A Heart Never Dies*. Readers can contact Karen by email, karengbruce85@gmail.com, on Facebook/Instagram (Karen G. Bruce), or at www.karengbruce.com.

www.ingramcontent.com/pod-product-compliance
Lightning Source LLC
Chambersburg PA
CBHW020335260626
47156CB00004B/1544